The beach

and other stories

The beach

and other stories by

Paul Harman

2023

The stories in *The beach and other stories* are works of fiction. Names, characters, businesses, institutions, places, events and incidents are either the products of the author's imagination or used in a fictitious manner. Any resemblance to actual persons, living or dead, or actual events is purely coincidental.

Published in 2023 by Paul Harman
Gulgong, New South Wales, Australia.

Editing by Linda Nix AE

Cover image of the beach from an original photograph
© Copyright Bryan Cuttance, used with permission.
Hat image used under licence from Shutterstock ID 383438464.

Cover design, text design and production by
Golden Orb Creative: www.goldenorbcreative.com

Typeset in 12 pt Palatino

A National Library of Australia Cataloguing-in-Publication entry has been created for this title:

ISBN 9780645190724 (pbk)
ISBN 9780645190731 (ebook)

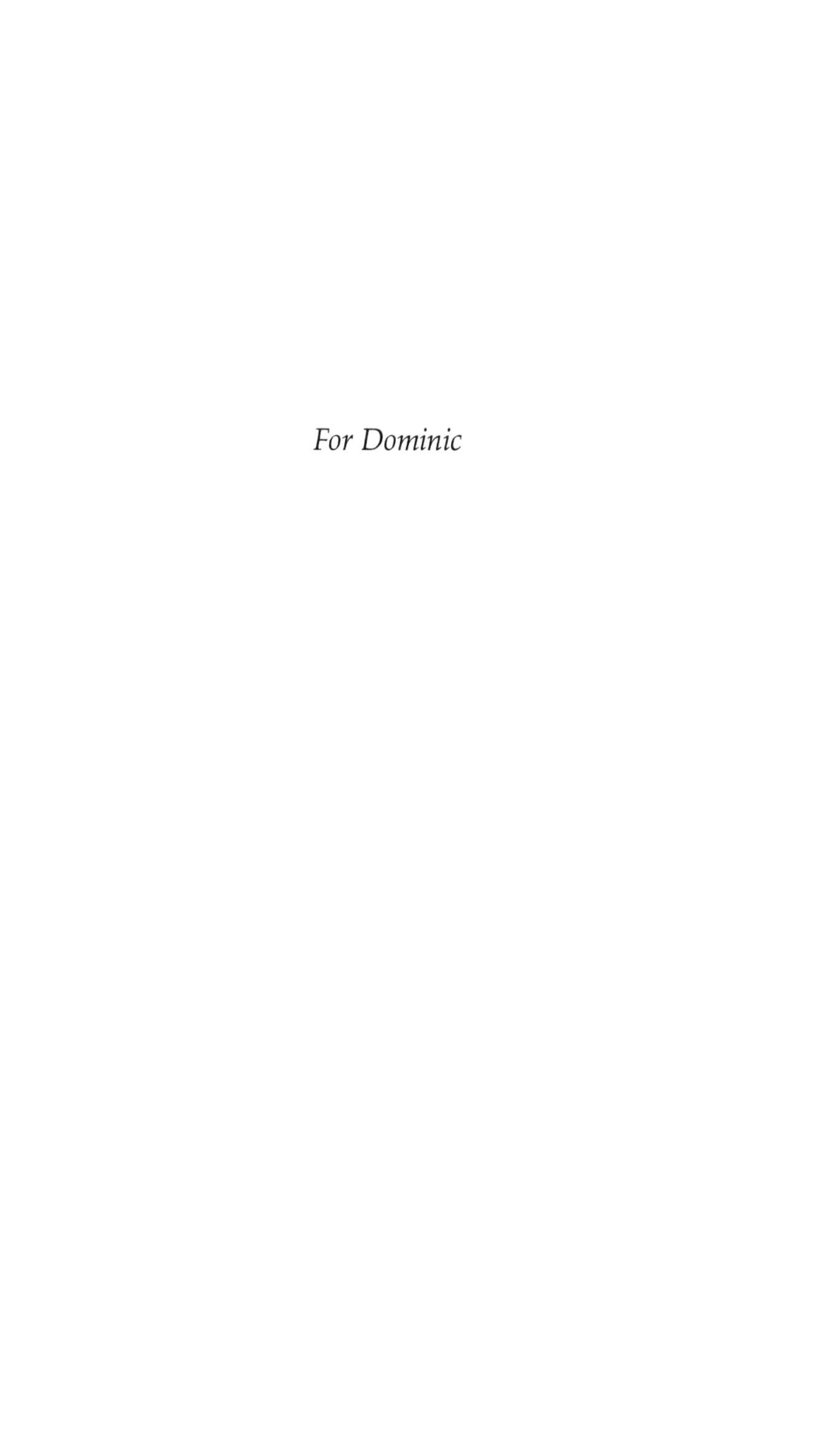

For Dominic

Contents

The beach

Shane Robinson stood at the shore. The rising sun blazed from beyond the horizon, and even though it was early in the morning, people were about, walking or riding their bikes along the pathways that ran along the foreshore. The café under the lifesaving club was already open, and locals were chatting to each other as they waited for their coffees. The water lapped at Shane's feet as the tide washed in. His toes sank into the wet sand as the water receded. The ocean looked sparkling and serene in the morning sun. There were swimmers in the water already, as well as surfers off the point at the other end of the beach.

Shane turned his head away from the beach and looked at the kiosk that jutted out from the foreshore. It was an open wooden structure, not very big, and had been around since the thirties. It wasn't really a kiosk as such – it didn't sell any snacks or ice creams – but locals had always called it the kiosk. It was more of a lookout. It had wooden seats so you could stop and have a sit-down as you looked out onto the ocean. For decades the kiosk had been a local landmark. It was a wonder it hadn't been knocked down with the development that was always going on in the area. The original surf club was built on the beach, and there were camping grounds on the beach for holiday-goers. In front of the kiosk, big black boulders rested on the sand, spat out from the ocean over thousands of years. Children and their parents would fossick amongst the rock pools for crabs and shells. The weather, including a few cyclones, had eroded the other sheds over time, and now all that was left besides the kiosk was the pavilion behind the beach. The pavilion housed the surf club and a pizza restaurant. It had a clock tower looking out to the ocean in the middle of the roof, a car park by the club and another one next to the pizza restaurant. Shane remembered when he was younger and living in another state, watching the telly seeing footage of the 1974 cyclone that hit southeast Queensland where the winds pushed the water all the way up to the pavilion.

But Shane wasn't standing on the beach for a bit of history revision. He was standing next to the groyne, which was a man-made formation built from tonnes of rock in the early seventies to control sand erosion. The groyne went out thirty or so metres from the shore. There were two groynes made at the beach, one at each end. The one he was standing next to was called the big groyne.

Shane was now in his thirties, was married, had children. He was on holidays visiting his parents and siblings, taking some rare time off from being a husband and a father. He was standing in his bathers, next to the groyne. He was on a mission.

Twenty-odd years back, when Shane was only about ten years old, he'd gone on a holiday with his sister to visit their grandparents. His parents had driven him and his sister to the airport, dropped them off with the airline staff and had packed them off to their grandparents for a fortnight.

He remembered crying with his sister in the boarding lounge when their parents left. Even though the airline staff were pleasant, it didn't stop both siblings from wailing their eyes out when their parents turned their backs and walked off. The tears soon dried up as the adventure of flying on a plane by themselves and holidaying near the ocean took over. It was a different world to the cold suburban lives they led down south. Their grandparents took them to restaurants, to pub dinners and to the golf club. There was a zoo and a racetrack behind where they lived, so every time they visited, they saw polar bears and lions and other zoo animals, and more often than not, after their visit to the zoo, they would have lunch with their grandparents while watching the trots at the racetrack.

One day their grandparents took Shane and his sister to the local beach. It was summer holidays; the beach was full of both tourists and locals enjoying a dip in the water. The beach back then was world-famous for its surf breaks and its legendary long barrels which attracted international surfers who competed in tournaments throughout the year. Shane and his sister spent the day dipping in and out of the water, hanging with their grandparents under the umbrella on the sand, lapping on ice-cream cones and drinking milkshakes. They had chips and hamburgers for lunch. Before they went home in the afternoon, Shane went for a swim on his own near the groyne. One last dip in the water. He splashed around a bit and then decided to head to the shore. But with each step he took, he found himself drifting out to sea. He tried to swim in but drifted further out to sea. He was caught in a rip. Every stroke he swam was just sending him further from the shore. The current was too strong for him. He had his feet in the sand, but the sand was moving with him. The shore was receding, he was panicking, he was losing energy and he was terrified, thinking he was going to drown. He'd gone out so far, the rip had pushed him near the tip of the groyne. He saw a man sitting on the rocks at its edge. The man had no top on, was only wearing shorts, and was drinking a bottle of beer in a brown paper bag while watching the waves roll in. Shane frantically waved to the man to get his attention. The man saw him, recognised Shane was in a bit of trouble, stood up and dived off a rock into the water and within seconds had Shane safely in his grasp. Together they swam to the safety of the groyne. They sat on the rocks for a moment as the man watched over the boy to make sure he was okay. Shane coughed up a bit of water but otherwise was fine. He thanked the man for his help, and then ran down the groyne to the beach. His saw his grandfather standing next to the umbrella, his hand protecting his eyes from the sun as he looked into the water, searching for his grandson. Shane snuck up behind his pa and tugged at his shorts and told him what happened. His grandfather was a relieved man as he comforted his grandson.

Twenty years later, Shane was back at the beach. His parents now lived in the same house as his grandparents had. His pa had died not long after that trip to the beach, and his parents had moved up north to look after his father's mother. His parents told him the news: the groyne was going to disappear. The council were going to rip it up. There was a sand containment issue across the border, and because of that the two groynes were going to be dug up and removed.

'But that groyne, the big one, that's where I almost drowned that time when I was at the beach with nan and pa,' Shane told his parents.

'Really?' his old man had said, rolling his eyes as he read his newspaper. 'That's the first I've heard of it.'

So the next morning, while his parents were still in bed, Shane was at the beach, holding onto a surfboard he had grabbed from his parents' garage. As the early morning joggers ran past and as the café-goers waited for their coffees, he started to tread into the water. His mission was to swim around the groyne before it was gone. Ever since that day when the rip carried him out and the man had to jump in from the groyne to save him, Shane had been terrified of water. He still swam in the ocean every time he flew up to visit his parents, but he swam between the flags and never went more than a few metres into the water. He was so terrified he was going to get taken by a rip again, he never ventured far into the ocean. His fear of the ocean was as deep as the water itself. Even though he lived in a country town, hundreds of kilometres from the coastline, he made sure his children took swimming lessons at his local aquatic centre. He didn't want them to suffer the same fear of water that he did.

Shane tightened his grip on the surfboard as he stepped closer to the water. He wanted to swim around the groyne before it disappeared to conquer his fear, to conquer his demons of the water. As he became older, he learnt he had to deal with many demons. But this was the one demon he had always wanted to conquer. His long-standing fear of the water. What better place to face it, Shane thought, than at the very spot where he nearly drowned?

Shane wasn't much of a swimmer, and couldn't surf to save himself; he was just going to use the board as a paddleboard to make things easier. It was a simple mission: paddle out to the tip of the groyne, go around it, and then paddle back on the other side. A sixty-metre trip. He had seen swimmers swim the width of the beach, which was hundreds of metres wide, on many occasions. What he had to do was simple. A five-minute journey, at most. It didn't feel like a simple mission, he thought, as he lowered the board and waded into the water.

The water was warm, calm and gentle, almost still. When the water was to his knees, Shane ran a few steps, and plunged into the water on top of his surfboard. The surfboard lunged forward with his weight and before he knew it, he was already ten metres out from shore. He used his hands to paddle out to sea further. The water was clean and translucent; he saw tiny schools of fish and shells stuck to the rocks underneath. A couple of early morning walkers were strolling on top of the groyne and looking out to the views of the ocean. In less than a minute he had paddled to the tip of the groyne. How easy was this, he thought. He saw the same rock his rescuer had been sitting on all those years back, drinking his bottle of beer, and even remembered which rocks they had climbed up after the man saved him. Shane reached the tip of the groyne, then turned his surfboard, paddled across the edge of the groyne, and tilted the board towards the shore.

He stopped paddling and sat up on the surfboard and looked beyond the sand and the beach to the road and the buildings. Seagulls soared above him, squawking as they flew in the breeze. He looked down and he saw his knees and legs under the water. He smiled as he wiggled his toes. They looked like worms on a fishing line.

He looked back up and beyond the shoreline. Tall Norfolk pine trees that lined the highway had been around for years. Things were always changing in the neighbourhood, but the trees were still there. The zoo behind the beach had gone, and in its place was a gated housing community.

A developer had wanted to close off the highway and build a resort for wealthy residents who had private access to the beach. There were community protests and from the negative feedback the developer shelved his grand plans. Shane looked beyond the highway. A lot was still as he remembered from when he was a kid. The art deco styled pub was still there, and a giant bronze eagle that sat on the hill behind the kiosk remained. The flats along the highway were no taller than two stories high. There was a petrol station, a post office, a milk bar, a chemist, a butcher and a charity shop on the highway. He remembered playing the pinball machines at the milk bar when he came up to visit his grandparents. He remembered the sound the pinball had made when he won a free game. A loud 'crack', like the sound of a whip, would ring out from the pinball speaker.

Shane felt a tinge of sadness as he straddled the surfboard. He turned to the ocean and saw through the haze across the water the outlines of high-rise buildings in the distance. With the groyne being removed, he felt the town was going to undergo change. The towers of the more famous towns up the other end of the coast would creep down like a long shadow. The ramshackle two- or three-storey weatherboard flats he was looking at would one day be replaced by much higher development blocks, and there would be nothing he could do about it.

The tide changed, and the ripples that Shane had paddled out into were turning into waves. Waves that were now cresting and crashing into the shore. Shane and his board rose up and down with the waves. He felt at peace, being on his own in the water as he lurched up and down. He felt no rush to head to the shore. Even if he had only travelled thirty metres out, he had conquered a fear. He lifted his head, closed his eyes and felt the sun on his face. He was happy. After a minute he leant down and rested his stomach on the board and started paddling into shore. One of the waves behind him was larger than the others. Shane furiously paddled his arms and legs, then as the wave started to break it carried him and his board all the way to the shore. He had a grin as big as his board as the water crashed over him. The board slipped out of his hands when he crunched into the sand. He tumbled over a few times, then, still smiling, he stood up and went to retrieve his board.

He carried the board under his arm as he walked across the top of the groyne, back to where he had entered the water, to grab his towel and dry himself off before heading home.

He saw his family standing there.

'What the hell?' he said to himself.

They were standing in the sand, waiting for him. There were his parents, his brother and sister, and their partners. Even his grandmother, now in her eighties, was there. They were laughing at him as he approached.

'What's going on?'

'When I told you about the groyne being removed,' his father began, 'and then an hour later I heard you rummaging through the garage and saw you come out with your brother's surfboard, I knew what you had in mind. I made some phone calls last night to Melinda and Andrew, spoke to your grandmother, and here we all are. Well done. It takes guts, what you did.'

'Seriously?' his brother Andrew, who surfed all the time, protested. 'I can go that far out in my sleep.'

They heard a commotion behind them. They all turned and saw council trucks pull up on the foreshore with big yellow bucket excavators strapped onto the trays. The groyne was soon to be pulled apart.

'Geez, council don't muck around when it comes to knocking things down,' his father commented.

Shane walked with his brother, their feet squeaking in the sand as they headed to the café under the surf club to get coffees for everyone. His brother had been surfing since he was a kid, had been sponsored by some of the local businesses when he was younger and knew every grain of sand on the beach.

'That was fun out there, even if it was quick,' Shane said.

‘It is fun out there,’ Andrew agreed. ‘How about after our coffees, we go out for a surf together? I’ll run back home and grab another board. What do you say?’

Shane looked back to the waves that were rolling in, the blueness of the water, the seagulls flying above the ocean. Dogs were running unleashed along the water; swimmers had left their towels clumped on the sand as they went for a dip. Members of the lifesaving club were setting up for their day of patrolling. His brother’s blond hair flowed in the breeze as they walked. Shane’s fear of the water was gone. He couldn’t wait to get back in.

‘We can hang ten. The waves are gnarly. It will be radical, bro,’ Andrew added, grinning.

Shane knew his brother was taking the piss out of his lack of knowledge about surfing, but he didn’t care.

‘That would be cool,’ Shane replied.

Peak hour

'You sure about this, baby?' Lilly said to her boyfriend, Mac.

'I know. I'm not feeling crash-hot about it myself,' Mac replied. 'But it's been one of those days. I just want to get home. We'll be fine.'

They were in the front seats of Mac's car, and they were heading from northern New South Wales back up to Brisbane. He was driving his souped-up Ford Falcon V8 XB 351 sedan. The air-conditioning unit had recently broken, so they had the windows down and their hair flowed in the breeze as they tried to cool down. Mac was in jeans and a black tee-shirt and was resting his elbow on the door as he drove. Lilly was sitting with her legs folded underneath her. She was wearing a denim shirt with the sleeves cut off and white shorts with bright red flowers on them; her thongs rested next to her handbag below on the car mat. The leather seats were sticking to her clothes as she sweated with the heat.

Lilly put her hand on Mac's where it was resting on the gearstick as he drove. Then she reached across and turned on the radio. She picked up a country music station and hummed along to a tune called 'Drunk on a Plane,' and tried not to worry. She bit her bottom lip as she stared out the windscreen to the road they were driving on. The white painted lines disappeared, one after the other, under the car.

'Okay, babe. Whatever you say. I'm sure we'll be fine,' Lilly said to Mac, without an ounce of confidence in her voice.

It had been a shit day for Mac. Everything that could have gone wrong, did go wrong. He worked for a drug kingpin in Brisbane, and once a fortnight he drove down to Byron Bay and bought somewhere between five and ten pounds of marijuana, which he then drove back up to Brisbane for his boss. It was easy money for Mac. The money he made paid for his rent, his university courses, and he only had to work a couple of days a fortnight. That was the best bit. While his mates at university had to scramble to balance lectures with part-time work, Mac had an easy gig. The catch though, was obvious. If he was busted with a huge stash of marijuana in his car, he'd be facing jail time. And if he blabbed, and told the police who he worked for, things would be a whole lot tougher than just doing a stint in Boggo Road. Besides marijuana, his boss shipped amphetamines, cocaine and heroin all over the country. Mac stayed away from being involved in the harder drugs. He didn't even smoke. He just paid his rent, read his books, attended his courses, and then once a fortnight, he'd disappear for forty-eight hours. Mac was at the lower rung in the ladder in the drug business. He was a little fish in a big river, though his role was one of the more important ones. He was the transport.

No one knew about his secret job, except his girlfriend. He had met Lilly a couple of months back at a party at Redcliffe; they'd hit it off, and they'd been living in each other's pockets ever since. You could keep your secret job as a drug runner from your family and your house mates, but not your girlfriend. She had quickly got suspicious of his fortnightly trips away, and asked if he had another girlfriend over the border, so Mac came clean.

Mac adhered to a very strict routine. He left Brisbane in the mornings and drove straight through to Byron Bay. Every cop in town could pull him over if he wanted to on the way down. They could pull the car apart if they wished. There'd be nothing to find. He'd get to Byron, buy the marijuana off the usual dealer, then divide the trip back to Brisbane into two parts. First he'd stay overnight around Southport at the top end of the Gold Coast. He varied where he stayed, just in case someone was onto him. Not that there were many accommodation options in Southport. There was a motel on the highway and a caravan park by the Nerang River. Such was his paranoia, he'd demand different rooms at the motel, and different caravans at the park with each visit. Then he'd peel back on the highway in the early morning and head back up to Brisbane along with the many morning workers who travelled the eighty or so kilometres from the Gold Coast every day to Brisbane for work. Travelling back from Byron, through the Gold Coast, then back to Brisbane and onto the drop-off point was the riskiest part of Mac's trip. Mac used the other cars around him as they commuted to work as protection from the police. Be one of many. It was a bit hard around Byron Bay to blend in as there wasn't as much traffic, but he had never come across any highway patrol cars in northern New South Wales. Mac's rule of thumb was, don't drive at night, travel with the peak hour.

The car he drove wasn't exactly an unassuming family car like everyone else drove. It didn't blend in at all. The Ford had belonged to his father, and Mac inherited it when he died. When Mac drove through the streets of Coorparoo where he lived, there was no prouder man. The extractors fitted to the car made it rock from side to side as it sat in traffic. It was painted a dark metallic blue with black stripes down the sides. It rumbled and throbbed, was as loud as a jet plane, was just as thirsty, but could go like lightning when Mac wanted it to. It was a true muscle car. It stood out from the sedans and station wagons, but when he hit the outer suburbs of Brisbane where the traffic banked up, Mac needed the comfort of the other cars around him to avoid detection. He needed a buffer, a security blanket from the cops if they were around. He'd thought about hiring a Nissan or a Holden, something average that blended in with the other traffic that the police wouldn't glance at. But he decided to stick with his souped-up Ford Falcon, just in case something did come up, and he needed the power of the V8. So, every fortnight for nearly a year, Mac had driven from Brisbane to Byron, timing his return back to Brisbane with the congestion of the morning peak hour on the city's southern outskirts.

He had a bad feeling when Lilly asked to come with him. She was breaking his routine, but he couldn't say no to her. He explained the risks, but she still was keen. He should have put his foot down and said no, but then he thought he could take her to a nice restaurant when he stayed overnight at his usual place in Southport. Maybe go to Surfers. Sit on the beach and watch the waves roll in. Spoil Lilly a bit.

So, they left Brisbane at the same time as he always left. About nine am. The sun was up, the day was already hot and humid. Mac filled the car with petrol just out of Brisbane, then they headed down to Byron.

Things started going amiss when they reached the pickup point in Byron. Mac usually met the dealer at a café. They'd have a coffee together, make some polite chit-chat, then Mac would pass an envelope stuffed full of cash under the table, and they'd walk outside to the dealer's car. The dealer had the drugs in a satchel in the boot. Mac would scan the car park to see if there was anyone suspicious lurking about, then pick up the satchel, say 'See you next time' to the dealer, walk to his car and head out of Byron. But after thirty minutes of Lilly reading the menu for the hundredth time and Mac looking out the window wondering what the hold-up with his dealer was, Mac ran out of patience. He left Lilly at the café on her own and went to find a public telephone so he could ring his boss.

'Mac,' his boss said down the line. 'What took you so long? There's been a change in plans.'

He was told to go to a pub in Byron. Some people were waiting for him; his boss had told them what Mac looked like. They would seek him out and he could do the exchange there instead.

The dealers at the pub when he met them weren't the usual dealers. They were loud, brash, showing off to each other. They seemed to be tripping and he had trouble understanding what they were talking about. A born-again Christian kept pestering Mac and Lilly to come for a free meal at his local church. The dealers weren't very discreet, and they were more interested in playing pool and chatting up Lilly, trying to get her drunk, than selling him drugs. The dealers kept on changing the rules with every passing game of pool, which added to his frustration. Mac held the pool cue in his hand, trying to stay calm, trying to suppress the urge to smash his cue over these dickhead amateur drug dealers. Normally he would be in Byron for about twenty minutes. Instead, he was held up for over three hours. Eventually though, the deal was done, and he bought six pounds of marijuana. He went to a secluded part of Byron with a couple of the dealers and secured the drugs.

When he finally had the gear, he divided the marijuana into six parts and wrapped each part in

Gladwrap to hide the smell. Then with a couple of screwdrivers Mac jimmied open the front two interior door panels of his Ford and stashed the gear inside the door. Queensland had just introduced tougher drug laws. He would definitely be sent to jail if he was caught. He would protect Lilly though. Nothing surer. She had nothing to do with it. But fingers crossed, he wouldn't have to worry about any of that.

On his way back, to add to the drama, the petrol station he usually stopped in at Kingscliff to fill up was closed, so he had to deviate along the back roads south of the Tweed River, searching for another petrol station. It took forever, driving on dimly lit country roads, before he found a petrol station at Chinderah. By the time he was back on the highway and had crossed the border back into Queensland, it was dark, he was way behind time, he had a thumping headache and he just wanted to go home. He shelved his planned romantic evening with Lilly on the Gold Coast. It would have to wait another time. He made his decision when he was on the Gold Coast Highway. Instead of taking the Bundall turnoff and driving to Southport for the night, he would risk going straight to Brisbane. The decision went against every form of discipline, every routine he'd abided by. There was no peak hour traffic at night-time. There was no buffer of bumper-to-bumper traffic to protect him. They were on their own. But it was settled. He would go straight through, back to Brisbane.

He told Lilly of his plan to head home. She felt like she was a bit of a curse for Mac. She was more worried that she had disrupted his travelling patterns than encountering any trouble with the police. They had been on the road for eight hours and she hadn't seen any police cars at all.

***

The song on the radio ended, and another country song began: 'Jesus Wasn't Born in a Hammock'. Mac tapped his fingers on top of the gearstick. Lilly grabbed her handbag, rifled around inside until she found her make-up case and pulled out her nail file. The Ford rumbled in the night. Mac didn't go over the speed limit. He didn't want to get pulled over for speeding and get done by bad luck. They were seventy kilometres from Brisbane. Mac tried to calm his nerves by listening to the radio, while Lilly looked out the window and filed her nails to pass the time.

Fifteen minutes later, they were fifty kilometres out of Brisbane. Mac kept looking at his watch. He couldn't help checking it every minute. When they were thirty kilometres out, Mac was starting to breathe a little bit easier. The traffic was quiet and there were no cops around at all. They rose over a hill on the motorway and the lights of Brisbane's CBD beckoned in front of them. Mac looked at his watch again. It was 8:05. He did his sums. They should be back at his place in about twenty-five minutes and rolling the Ford into the garage at 8:30. He paid a bit extra in rent because he liked to keep his car out of the weather so the sun couldn't crack the dashboard or take the shine off the paint. When they drove past an aquarium store ten minutes later, Mac didn't have to look at his watch. He knew where he was. He knew he was only fifteen kilometres from home. Then the speed limit changed, and Mac geared down. He smiled. They had hit the city limits. With each kilometre they travelled, Mac felt a load lift off his shoulders. Not much was happening on a slow weeknight in Brisbane. When a new song played on the radio, 'Your Parlour is my Home', Mac whistled along to the tune. He turned to Lilly and winked at her.

'I think we're good, baby,' he reassured his girlfriend, although he was reassuring himself more. He took his hand off the gearstick and stroked Lilly's leg. 'We'll be home in ten minutes.'

Lilly smiled at him. As Mac went to turn back and face the highway, something caught his eye. They were driving past a service station. In the parking bay outside was a police patrol car.

Two policemen were on a break and were walking from their squad car into the service station. They stopped at the doors when they heard Mac's Ford and spun around. Mac and Lilly stared in panic at the cops for a split second. It was long enough for the two police officers to abandon their plans to enter the servo, and they started running back to their car.

'Oh, fuck,' Lilly groaned. 'Oh, fuck.'

Mac gunned it. That's all he could do. Hope they could outrun the cops. They weren't too far away, only one suburb from where Mac lived. They were so close. A new song started on the radio station. 'A Rollercoaster of Love.' Mac wasn't in the mood for country music anymore and switched the radio off. He felt he was on a rollercoaster of his own making. He didn't slow down as he drove over a large hill on the main road that led to his suburb. He was doing 100 in a 60 zone. He drove over the second hill just as the cops had reached the top of the first hill. Mac looked in the rear-view mirror. He saw the flashing lights of the police car and he could hear the sirens in the distance. There was one final hill to overcome. A steep and sloping hill. Mac gunned it and the Ford zoomed up the hill. He went so fast that when the reached the top, the Ford became airborne. Lilly screamed, and they bounced up and down in their seats when they landed, and there were sparks from the undercarriage as it hit the asphalt. When they bottomed out, Mac slowed down and killed the lights. The larger hill offered protection from the police, blocking their line of sight. They were only a minute from his house. The police were too far away. The power of his car pulled them through. Mac hooked left off the main road, then turned right and drove past rows of houses. Then he slowed to a crawl and turned into the driveway of his house. They had made it. He took deep breaths, and his heart pumped a little slower. He idled the Ford in neutral as he reached across Lilly and opened the glovebox. He ran his fingers along the bottom of the glovebox rummaging through the rego papers, spare fuses and light globes. He found the remote for the garage roller door, clicked the button and the door began to rise.

Their joy was short-lived. One of Mac's housemates was moving out, and the garage was full of cardboard boxes stuffed with his soon to be ex housemate's belongings. Mac had forgotten all about it.

'Fucken fuck.'

He turned the car off and they both ran into the garage. He switched the garage light on and for the next few minutes, they were frantically stacking boxes on top of each other against the wall as they created space for the Ford. When there was enough room Mac ran back down the driveway to the car. He saw at the intersection at the top of the street a car was slowly making its way down the road. He saw a flashlight coming from the patrol car sweeping the driveways and the cars parked on the street. He started the Ford, let the clutch out and drove into the garage. A new problem arose. He couldn't find the remote control for the roller door. It must have slipped under one of the seats when he had sped into the garage. He raced from the car to the front of the garage and thumped the back of his hand against the control panel and the roller door slowly started to come down. He turned the light of the garage off and Mac crouched with Lilly in front of the car as the roller door, inch by inch, cranked its way down to the floor. It seemed to take forever. It was torturous to watch. It wasn't until the lip of the roller door touched the concrete and the motor whirled to a stop that they breathed a sigh of relief.

The Ford was cooling down. The engine crackled and the room smelt of burning oil. The chrome from the mag wheels and the front bumper glistened in the darkness.

Mac looked across to Lilly. She was quiet, still, not daring to move.

Mac had thought he was a cool dude going to university and making easy money doing a drug run once a fortnight. What a fool he was, he thought now. Mac thought about the thing he would have missed the most if he was in jail. He wouldn't miss his classes, he wouldn't miss his housemates and he wouldn't miss his Ford Falcon. He would miss Lilly. Outside they heard the tyres of the police car roll in front of Mac's house. They could hear the garbled voice of the dispatch announcer on the police radio.

Mac turned to Lilly. 'Will you marry me?' he whispered.

The police car stopped. They could see the beam of the yellow spotlight shine in the gap under the roller door. It flickered from side to side, disappeared for a second or two, and then shone back on the garage door again.

Mac saw Lilly's eyes widen at his surprise proposal. He would give up everything to be with Lilly. He could sell his Ford Falcon and move interstate with her. Somewhere far away. Somewhere near the beach. Broome maybe. He pictured the pair of them riding the camels at sunset on Cable Beach. He had saved up a fair chunk of cash. He wasn't worried about university – he could defer his courses if he wanted to. The cops chasing them, even if it was only for a few minutes, had scared Mac straight. He was done with being a drug mule. He didn't want to feel that hopelessness and that fear ever again. He wanted to be with Lilly. That's all he wanted. He knew that now.

'What did you say?' Lilly whispered back to him in a disbelieving tone. 'You want to marry me?'

The flash from the torch finally disappeared. The voice of the dispatcher faded as the police car rolled down to the next house. They were safe. Mac stood up, went to the workbench behind him and rummaged around in his toolbox, then he crouched back down next to Lilly. In his hand was a large, galvanised washer. Mac picked up Lilly's left hand and slipped the washer onto her wedding finger.

'What do you say? Will you marry me?' Mac asked Lilly again, a bit more nervously than the first time.

Three greyhounds

Like a lot of other young people, I was unsettled in my teens, and just as unsettled as a young adult, and I drifted in and out of many friendships. I had no direction in life, but really wasn't looking for any. When Gerald appeared on the scene I began to focus, and for a while, with Gerald in my life, I found a new direction.

I worked in the warehouse for Target at Tweed Heads when I was offered a similar job at the Southport store. My pay as a receiving clerk was to be the same; I had to travel further to work, so to me it didn't seem much of a promotion. I said yes to the transfer only because I couldn't think of a plausible reason to say no, and was flattered to an extent that I was headhunted. Though, I'm not sure if I made a great impression on my first day.

In the lead-up to my transfer, the manager from Southport, Mr Dutton, had phoned me. One of his strict store policies, he told me, was for his employees to wear trousers and not jeans. Introduced no doubt, because of the laid-back beach culture that infiltrated many facets of life on the Gold Coast. I forgot all about his trouser policy and walked in on my first day wearing faded blue denim jeans. I bumped into Mr Dutton on the staircase when I was being shown around and he frowned when he noticed I wasn't in trousers. He cut short my tour, directed me to the men's clothing section and I was given ten minutes to buy myself a pair of trousers.

All the sales reps in the store were known only by their surnames. Mr Dobell worked in outdoor and hardware, Miss Bennett was in fabrics and sewing, and Mr Bray was in charge of electronics. The man in gardening was my age and it felt stupid calling him Mr Kedwell so all the workers just called him Danny. Such dignities didn't exist for the rest of the staff. My nametag simply read 'Joe'. Mr Lynch worked in stationery. He lived five minutes away so he would go home for his lunch break and would return chewing gum to hide the smell of beer on his breath. If he had too much to drink he would nap in the fixtures out the back. My supervisor from the receiving office, Mrs Ashton, had known Mr Lynch since they were children. 'He's had a tough life that one,' she told me once when he stumbled down towards the back of the fixtures. She would turn the store music down so he could sleep, and then cover for him on the floor until he woke up.

The store was flooded with casual workers just out of school to help with the run-up to Christmas. Target did a national stocktake twice a year where every single item on the floor and out the back was counted. If we were running late, management would lock us in and not let us leave until it was all done. At the Tweed Heads store, frustrated parents, sick of waiting outside in their cars until well after dark, would bang on the roller doors, calling out for their son or daughter.

When I started in October, the day of the stock-market crash, the speaker located above my desk was already playing Christmas carols. Target skimped on the song royalties as only five carols were played over and over again. Being a receiving clerk for Target wasn't exactly a glamorous calling but I was twenty, still living at home and had no commitments. My desk was located near the back dock and when the trucks arrived with their deliveries I'd lift the roller door. I'd have the pallets ready and the truck driver would help me unload the goods.

My job was making sure that all the recently delivered new stock was accounted for. I'd tick everything off against the manifest, then stamp and sign the packing slips for the admin ladies. Their office was next to my desk and I would slide open the small window and hand through my paperwork for processing after each delivery.

Gerald was one of four storemen who floated in and out the front and back helping the sales reps, assisting customers, stocking the shelves or helping me at the dock when the distribution centre sent a semi-trailer full of goods.

I saw a bit of Gerald as he waltzed in and out in his blue coat, jeans and desert boots. One day during a lull after a spate of deliveries, Gerald was on the bludge; he came up to me for a chat and we found out we both came from Melbourne. 'Who ya barrack for, then?' he asked. Gerald was Footscray and I was Carlton. Not for the first time a friendship blossomed based on the love of Aussie rules.

Gerald lived in a caravan at the racetrack just down the road from me in Kirra. He raced greyhounds which were kennelled at the racetrack and the managers gave him cheap rent in one of the caravans on the grounds. He lived in an eighteen-foot Millard caravan with the axles resting on Besser blocks. There was a bed at one end, a table with bench seats at the other near the door, and a bar fridge under the sink full of nothing but Coca-Cola. Gerald was the only bloke I knew amongst our circle of friends, besides me, who didn't drink alcohol. There were framed photos of his greyhounds competing in races hanging on the wall. Our mateship was fast-tracked when I found out that he lived so close to me. He had a car, I didn't, so he drove me to work every day.

I found out that Gerald had a bit of a mean streak about him, inconsistent with his usual cheerful manner. One day while I was hanging with him and some friends in his caravan, he rummaged through a cupboard up the top and pulled out a shotgun. In one quick movement he aimed the barrels squarely at my head and pulled the trigger. *Click.* There were no bullets of course. I'm pretty passive and knew he was just showing off. There were other people in the caravan, and I laughed along with everyone else.

One morning I was a bit late getting to the caravan park to get my lift to work and Gerald berated me as I hopped into his car. 'How dare you keep me waiting?' he thundered, spit bursting from his mouth. He lectured me about punctuality until we were well past Tugun. I let him have his tirade. I had always been timid and let Gerald get it out of his system. I looked at the clock on the dashboard when I had closed the door and was putting my seat belt on – I was three minutes late. He was usually just as mild-mannered as me but I was an easy mark when he got angry. Back then I didn't talk back much. There are worse things than being yelled at by a mate, although it can be said mates shouldn't feel the need to yell at you over a trivial matter or pull the trigger on a gun pointed at your head.

We didn't have girlfriends; we weren't mature enough anyway but, looking back, we really just weren't that interested. Maybe the choice had been made for us. Gerald was skinny and gangly with thinning red hair that was parted on the side, and the tip of his nose leant across to his left cheek. I'd had acne since I was fourteen. My cheeks and chin were pockmarked, which put paid to any brewing confidence that might have emerged as I got older. We both dropped out of school early, didn't have much of an education, even less of an imagination. We knew our limitations. It was sport that bonded us as friends.

When the Boxing Day Test match was on in December 1987, we hid from management in the electronics department one afternoon watching the cricket on the TV screen. Mike Whitney blocked the last ball of the final over against the bowling of Kiwi supremo Richard Hadlee to save a Test match for the Aussies. We crouched down among the radio-cassette players and Sony Walkmans in the audio cabinets, ducking our heads up occasionally like prairie dogs to see if management were onto us. A jubilant Whitney and his batting partner Craig McDermott hugged in the middle of the pitch, celebrating like they had just scored the winning runs to clinch the World Cup.

The temptation of being in Melbourne for the start of the new footy season was enough for us to quit our jobs, pack it all in and drive the 1700 kilometres south over the Australia Day weekend in 1988. We simply decided that we'd move to Melbourne together to watch the footy.

When we were bored at work and when we were on our own in the fixtures at the back, we mimicked the commentary of 3AW legends Harry Beitzel and Tommy Lahif to pass the time. We remembered the fun we'd had going to matches when we lived in Melbourne, watching games, following the exploits of our favourite players. I loved football and couldn't wait to go. I had followed my mother's footsteps and supported Carlton. When we lived in Melbourne I had seen premierships, stood in the outer in Princes Park marvelling at the skills of champions such as Ashman, Jesaulenko, Mackay, Johnstone and Silvagni. I had a jumper Mum bought me before I had even started school that was my most prized possession. I loved the navy blue, the monogram on the front. As soon as I was old enough I went to every game I could. When we moved to Queensland I would sit with Mum in the lounge and watch the match of the day beamed in from Melbourne, regardless of who was playing. 1987 was a good year. Carlton won the premiership, running away from Hawthorn on a sweltering day at the MCG.

So, Gerald and I gave two weeks' notice on the same day. We had nowhere to stay in Melbourne, or jobs lined up, trifling matters that didn't worry us. My parents ho-hummed about it all, thinking that they could count the weeks until I rang up begging for money to get home. They underestimated me. I loved football and couldn't wait to go.

Gerald had a Ford Falcon panel van, which we were going to drive to get to Melbourne. His greyhounds were coming too and he had vague plans to stop at race meets along the way to enter his dogs with the hope he might pick up some quick prize money. It was the middle of summer so we decided to avoid the heat of the inland roads and travel the Pacific Highway for the coastal breezes, then skirt the outer suburbs of Sydney before connecting with the Hume Highway which would take us to Melbourne. We were going to drive straight through. That was the plan. We knew we wouldn't be able to find any accommodation that would take Gerald's greyhounds.

Gerald picked me up from my home in Kirra on the Saturday morning. I had already said goodbye to my dad who was at work but my mother came out to meet Gerald and see me off. Both Gerald and I had brought a bag stuffed with clothes and they were thrown in the back with the greyhounds. Mum looked into the back of the Ford panel van, saw three panting greyhounds resting on blankets and burst into laughter. Perhaps out of pity she slipped fifty dollars into my hands as we hugged and said our farewells. My brother had won a sponsorship from Kirra Surf and was surfing at Duranbah, so it was my sister who stood with my mother waving us off from the driveway. I wound down the window and I blew my mother and sister kisses all the way down Coolangatta Road until they faded from view.

I had travelled on buses from the Gold Coast to Melbourne a few times over the years. I could think of better ways to spend twenty-six hours, cooped up next to someone you didn't know, watching B-grade videos with sore and cramped legs. The buses always ran late and twenty-six hours became twenty-eight or twenty-nine so I didn't have a problem sharing driving duties with Gerald with his three greyhounds in the back for a long period of time.

We decided to do eight-hour turns behind the wheel. It was a three-speed manual; I only had an automatic licence but wasn't worried. I'd been driving manuals long before I got my licence. The weather was scorching even though it was early morning. Gerald took first shift and we crossed the border into New South Wales in three minutes. That was the easy part. The next border crossing at Albury on the Murray River was about sixteen hours away.

It wouldn't have mattered which highway we took, it was impossible to avoid the heat. Gerald's air conditioner had a minimal effect as the outside heat enclosed the car so we had the windows down for most of the way. He soon abandoned the notion of entering his dogs in any races. Being cooped up in furnace-like conditions in the back was hardly ideal preparation.

We survived on pies, pasties and Cokes bought whenever we pulled in for petrol. We stopped every hour to give water to the dogs and we stopped if we saw a park off the highway so the dogs could have a walk. It was slow going with the dogs. Gerald fretted over them and he was always looking in the rear-view mirror to check on them.

We had a routine every time we stopped for petrol. We'd wash ourselves in the bathroom, stock up on food and give the dogs an amble around the petrol station.

The first drama we faced was getting a flat tyre just out of Byron Bay. We pulled to the shoulder of the road and hopped out to check the damage. I found out Gerald was as hopeless with mechanics as me. He had no jack or tools for the simple act of changing a tyre. He waited till he saw another Ford approaching, then flagged the driver so we could borrow his tools. The driver and Gerald stood at the back of the Falcon and chatted away as I sweated on the ground on all fours, flies buzzing around me as I changed the tyre, while cars jetted past, spraying loose gravel and hot fumes in their wake. When I finished changing the tyre I asked Gerald if he had checked the oil before we left. He mumbled he didn't so I popped the bonnet. I showed our good Samaritan the dipstick. There wasn't much oil in the engine. He shook his head, mumbled to himself as he went to his car, and pulled out a container of Valvoline for us.

It was dusk by the time we got to the turnoff to Port Macquarie and it was my turn to take over the wheel. Gerald opened the back and jumped in with his dogs, used his bag as a pillow and promptly fell asleep. I put my snacks and drinks next to me, slipped the car into gear and headed back onto the highway to drive through the night. After a while, it became a blur in the darkness but I was on a good stretch of highway so I felt confident with my driving. I just followed the white lines in the middle as I navigated the bends and the dips. I played chicken with the trucks when they rushed up from behind. When I stopped near Forster to refuel I heard the night-time singing of crickets and the mating calls of cicadas. I saw turtles trying to cross the highway near Newcastle.

Gerald slept through the night with his beloved greyhounds. Their names were Hunting Oscar, Bluebell and Night Time Bliss. Hunting Oscar was the pick of the three. He had placed at Capalaba, Ipswich and Murwillumbah. They panted over Gerald as he snored. I watched in the rear-view mirror as the dogs drooled into his open mouth. When that happened Gerald would cough a little, toss and turn a bit, then he would shift back to the same position, with his mouth open and the dogs hovering above him. I gave up looking after the fourth time it happened. I hit the Hume Highway at Liverpool in Sydney's western suburbs just after four in the morning. Gerald woke when I stopped at Narellan. We cleaned the back of the panel van, got rid of the dog's piss and shit, shook the blankets clean and Gerald gave the dogs a run while I filled up.

I tried to stay awake for Gerald as he drove. The dogs were restless so we kept on stopping to stretch their legs and most of the day was spent on the side of the road or at parks or the streets behind petrol stations, giving his greyhounds another walk. I had a quick nap between Gundagai and Tarcutta. When we crossed the border into Wodonga, to celebrate arriving in Victoria we bought some Kentucky Fried Chicken for dinner. The dogs smelt the chicken, couldn't resist and poked their heads between our seats, licking their lips. They were dehydrated and dripping in sweat. We fed them chunks of chicken and they licked our fingers clean when we finished.

I refused to sleep in the back with the dogs so I drifted in and out of sleep in the passenger seat while Gerald drove. I woke once to find the car idling with Gerald doing star jumps in the middle of a lone stretch of highway. The high beams silhouetted his figure. He looked like he was warming up for a gymnastics demonstration. 'What the fuck, Gerald?' I yelled to him as he sheepishly ran back to the car. We sang Rick Astley songs at the top of our voices with the windows down when we hit Seymour. When we passed through Kilmore and we could see the lights of Melbourne, we did our football impersonations. Smokey Dawson, Tommy and Harry. Jack Dyer, Skeeter Coughlan. We made a bet at Campbellfield that the first one to spot a tram wins ten dollars. We got to Coburg at eleven and we saw the last tram for the night being driven to the depot. 'Saw it first,' said Gerald. 'You owe me ten bucks!' he cried jubilantly.

We turned off Sydney Road shortly after and reached my brother's house in Brunswick. All the lights were off; we knocked and got no answer so I assumed he was out somewhere. He knew we were coming but hadn't told me where the spare key was so we drove around until we found a phone booth. Gerald rang his father, Bruce, who buzzed us into his unit in Prahran after we'd driven across town. His father had played a few games in the reserves for Geelong in the early sixties before his knees gave way. We slept on the lounge-room floor with the dogs locked in the laundry. Bruce's wife cooked us breakfast then Gerald started arguing with him at the kitchen table. He had a tempestuous relationship with his father. When I had first met Gerald, he'd told me that, years back when he was living with his girlfriend, his father moved in with them for a while. Gerald went to visit his mother in Ballarat one weekend and came back to find his girlfriend had moved out of Gerald's room and had shacked up with his father. They had been arguing ever since.

I finished my food, grabbed my bag and left. I hugged Gerald goodbye as he walked me downstairs and we both promised to catch up soon. I caught two trams to my brother's house where I was going to stay until I got settled, then move out on my own. The opposite happened. I cleaned out one of the spare rooms and ended up living there for a while.

Gerald and I didn't catch up as much as we'd thought, and I didn't go to the football at all. I joined a band so, instead of going to the footy, I was getting stoned most weekends in a garage in North Carlton. I discovered the taste of alcohol, wondered why it had eluded me for so long and spent a lot of my spare time sitting at the front bars of pubs around Brunswick and Fitzroy. My skin levelled out. I could finally talk to girls; I made new friends and played some gigs. I had a talent for music, and I was a natural on the bass guitar. I could write melodies which my band mates turned into songs. Footy wasn't important anymore. It turned out music, and the drugs and alcohol that came with it, had a greater leverage on me than Aussie rules ever did. There were notes left on the kitchen table for me that my brother had scribbled down for me when I was out. Phone calls I had missed, and they were all from Gerard, asking me to ring him. I never replied. For a long time there would be at least four messages a week waiting for me, then slowly it dwindled down to two or three a week, then the messages stopped coming altogether.

I was home one Saturday afternoon, reclining in my brother's chair, practising a riff on my bass that I had in my head and was trying to bring out through my fingers. In the background, the news was on the telly. The sports report commenced. I half listened as the reporter mentioned Footscray champion Doug Hawkins was playing his 200th game for Gerard's beloved Bulldogs.

I looked up as the highlights reel began and watched a grinning Hawkins burst through the banner at the MCG in front of his teammates. Then my jaw dropped, my fingers fell from my guitar. I spotted Gerald on the ground with his Footscray scarf around his neck standing with members of the cheer squad, with a camera in his hand taking pictures to mark the occasion, applauding, and with a big smile on his face as Hawkins and his teammates jogged past him. Only Gerald could wangle his way past officials onto the ground. The MCG no less.

'Fuck me, you stupid, stupid fool,' I cursed myself. Gerard might point a gun at my head and pull the trigger, but I could be just as cruel and heartless. Because I had an ear for music and a song, because I had learnt how to dress and because I had learnt not to be awkward around other people, did that justify me cutting Gerard off like I did? I knew the answer before I had even asked myself the question.

I rested my guitar against the chair, walked to the kitchen and grabbed my phone book.

Election day

I rocked up to the school just after eight on Saturday morning. It was the middle of March, the clouds and drizzle from the breaking dawn had cleared, and the sun hit my face as I walked the short distance from the bus stop. There were hives of people grouped around the entrance. I could smell onions and sausages cooking; parents were manning the BBQ outside the school hallway which had been converted to a voting booth. The polls for the 1993 federal election had just opened. I made my way to the Labor Party organiser by the gate and introduced myself.

'Suzie? I'm Julian. I'm rostered on to help with the how-to-vote pamphlets.' Suzie was in her fifties and had a straight freckled nose, blue eyes and a beaming moon-faced smile. She was wearing a tee-shirt with a picture of the prime minister emblazoned across it. There were banners for the Labor Party strung up on the wire gate behind her. Picture boards for the local candidate had yet to be rolled out, and instead leant against the fence next to boxes of voting materials. A thermos protruded from the top of Suzie's handbag, and underneath that were some fruit and sandwiches. During the week, I'd rung up Labor Party head office and volunteered myself for a couple of hours to help them out on election day. Suzie was the party coordinator for the polling booths around the electorate. She had my details on a clipboard with the day's roster and ticked my name off. She handed me a hundred or so how-to-vote pamphlets. Thin and wafer-like, the pamphlets showed a picture of the local candidate on the front with the voting preferences numbered one to six, and on the back was a glossy portrait picture of the prime minister, Paul Keating, in a black suit, cheekily smiling with gleaming white teeth.

'Where do you want me to go?'

'The Liberal volunteers haven't turned up yet. They must be running late, they haven't claimed a spot, so I guess you can pick anywhere you like.'

'Cool. What do you think of our chances today?'

'Oh, I don't know. I've heard there's been a bit of a swing back to us. Especially in Victoria, because of what Kennett has done, but it will be hard.' She raised her hands and showed me crossed fingers. 'We can only hope.'

A male voter wearing black sunglasses and with his hands deep in his pockets walked past us. He wore a scowl of anger and inconvenience. He spotted Suzie's tee-shirt.

'Fuck Labor,' he yelled at Suzie, as he stormed past us to the booths.

'We can only hope,' Suzie repeated to me, still smiling, but with a little less conviction.

There was another Labor volunteer standing by the main road, so I walked in the other direction to the end of the turning circle where parents dropped their kids off for school.

I passed volunteers for the minor parties standing in front of the fence: the Democrats, Greens, Christian Democratic Party, Grey Power. I received nods from all of them. Different politics, but brethren in party loyalty on polling day. I saw a couple of voters walk towards me. I held the pamphlets in one hand, licked my fingers with my other, and waited for them.

'Vote Labor, vote Labor, vote Labor,' I mumbled quickly as they approached. A man and a woman stopped and each grabbed a pamphlet from me. Their small white dog sniffed at my feet; the leash and the dog became tangled between my legs for a minute, then they wandered away from me to the school.

I recalled the conversation from Suzie a few minutes back: *'The Liberal volunteers haven't turned up yet.'*

I'd had no interest in politics until the state election the year before. Jeff Kennett was swept into power and things had changed in a very short time. Public schools had already been sold off and were going to be demolished to make way for residential development. Around 7,000 teachers were going to lose their jobs. There were going to be wide-ranging cuts to services and public transport; the TAB and the Gas and Fuel Corporation were to be privatised; councils were being forced to amalgamate; and every Victorian was going to pay a 100-dollar levy to get the state debt down. After 28 years of political apathy, I learnt a bit about Australian politics because of Jeff Kennett. I read up on the Whitlam years, John Curtin, Billy Hughes, Robert Menzies. I learnt of 200 years of deep-grained, in-built conservatism. Apartheid in South Africa was based partly on the gerrymander system that operated in Queensland. The Liberals introduced preferential voting in the 1920s to avoid three-corner voting contests, which benefited themselves and their coalition partner, the National Party, at the expense of the Labor Party. John Curtin, a beloved leader, died at his desk a few weeks before the war ended. Add the bizarreness of a prime minister disappearing while having a dip in the ocean, and a governor-general sacking the prime minister while the leader of the opposition was waiting in another room to be sworn in, made me wonder why I hadn't become interested in politics earlier.

When the largest protest since the Vietnam War took place in Victoria a month after the state Liberal Party was elected in November 1992, I had seen the light. It shone brightly, and I was the one of the 100,000 marchers who crammed the streets of the city.

With the upcoming federal election, I could see that what was happening in Victoria was going to be replicated across the country if John Hewson was elected. In the lead-up to the polls, with the Liberals holding a commanding lead, my manager would goad me good-naturedly at work. 'You're going to lose your leave loading; you're going to lose your leave loading …'

He wasn't wrong. If John Hewson was elected, in a pitch to small business, my leave loading and all the other leave loading of workers across the country would vanish. A goods and services tax would be introduced, Medicare would be abolished, and there was going to be a nine-month cap on unemployment benefits. After being in power for a decade, Labor was ripe for a bollocking. There was ten per cent unemployment across the country, a recession had crippled the economy, the media portrayed Paul Keating as full of hubris and arrogance, and according to the experts, voters were waiting for him with a big, recently sharpened axe. Labor had been behind in the polls before Keating toppled Hawke in 1991, and if recent events in Victoria had been anything to go by, by evening's end, Keating and Labor were going to be blasted into federal oblivion.

I liked Keating. He had a swagger; he seemed to believe in himself, had a bit of mongrel in him and wasn't swayed by the rabid opinions of the tabloids. He had never been popular though; he'd glibly fobbed off a recession as treasurer and, in a blokey nation of sports lovers, was widely pilloried for his love of antique clocks and classical music. He advocated Australia becoming a republic, embraced further ties in the Asia-Pacific region and introduced native title. Even to the true believers, he was hard to read, but he was one of us.

It was my admiration of Keating, more than my hostility towards the Liberal Party, that convinced me to give up my election day morning and help them out.

Solidarity.

The light on the hill.

It wasn't time.

A middle-aged man in blue overalls comes from around the corner.

'How you going, comrade?' he says in a cheery cigarette-ravaged voice.

He grabs a how-to-vote slip from me. He has black curly hair, olive skin and his fingers are caked in blue powder. A shift worker returning home after his stint in a nearby factory. When he returns five minutes later, he is chewing on a sausage sandwich, and he does the courtesy of returning the voting slip to me.

'Good luck, comrade,' he says to me in between mouthfuls.

The next voters are an elderly couple. They walk up arm in arm and they're dressed like they're off to a Sunday church service. When they see me holding a picture of Paul Keating on the voting slips, they make an arc and widen their space between me. I can't help myself.

'Vote Labor, vote Labor, vote Labor.'

It does me no good. They turn their noses up and continue strolling around me to the gate.

A family of four turn up: parents, with two surly, bored-looking teenage boys in tow.

'Vote Labor, vote Labor, vote Labor.'

'Vote Labor? Keating can go and get fucked,' the father says with fury in his voice. He taps his boys on their shoulders to get their attention, then points to me. 'If you ever vote for this mob, you're out of the house. Fucking eighteen per cent interest rates. Fucking one hundred per cent pricks.'

'Yes, dad,' the boys obediently mutter. The woman puts her arm over her husband's shoulder, trying to calm him down as they leave.

The boys shuffle behind their parents, hands in pockets, to the voting booths. They come back a few minutes later and the father speaks loudly to the mother as they walk past me, just to make sure I hear.

'Put the champagne on ice, honey. We'll save it for tonight.' The man glares at me a final time as they leave, to further make his point.

'The Liberal volunteers haven't turned up yet.'

In spite of the fury from the angry dad, I smile to myself. I committed my first act of political terrorism the night before. An act of spontaneity that was so brazen I can't believe I got away with it. I spent half the night in fear that my door was going to be beaten down, and the other half of the night laughing.

The candidate for the Liberal Party has his office in the street I live in. A one-storey red-brick building sandwiched between a bakery and a newsagent. I walked past it last night on my way home after work. The office was closed, but the blinds hadn't been pulled down, and in the dark, in the front of the office on a table by a wall, was all their promotional material wrapped up and neatly stacked ready for the election. The flyers, the banners, the corflutes with the candidate's picture on them, were all there. I stared at them. I thought of throwing a brick through the window and running down the street with the voting material under my arms. Instead, I thought of a better idea. I rushed to the supermarket, bought some glue, then returned to the office. I uncapped the glue with my mouth. It was a clear adhesive; I squirted half the container into the lock at the front door. Then I used my fingers to jam as much as I could further into the keyhole. Then I jumped the fence at the rear and did the same to the back door. Adrenaline kept me awake till after three in the morning. I slept in. I was supposed to meet Suzie at seven-thirty but I didn't arrive till after eight.

A young man in his mid-twenties comes up to me.

'Give me one of those pamphlets,' he demands. He's asked so nicely I give him two. He takes them from me and instead of heading inside, he heads back where he came from. I have no idea what he plans to do with them. A dart board with Paul Keating's face on it, maybe.

A man in his fifties with white hair and matching ponytail and beard comes up to me. He speaks to me in a thick Scottish brogue.

'I'll vote for your man, wee laddie.'

Most voters are quiet, polite and respectful, and most guard their voting intentions. They smile as they take the pamphlets from me, then go to the other parties and do the same before heading to the polling booths. I can't pick their voting loyalties. When they return the pamphlets to me, some give me a sly wink or a thumbs-up or a hopeful smile, revealing their allegiance to Labor.

A blue BMW pulls up outside the entrance, and a carload of Liberal volunteers scurry out. They look in a frantic state as they rush to the boot and grab their promotional material. They are all wearing identical freshly manufactured John Hewson tee-shirts. The eldest, a man in his sixties wearing sunglasses and cream-coloured jeans with shiny RM Williams boots, who I assume to be their coordinator, goes up to Suzie and begins an animated conversation with her. I see Suzie shaking her head in denial and he is still pointing his finger at Suzie as he retreats to help out his friends unload the car. Suzie gives him a wide-toothed smile and waves to him in a flippant manner, which further riles the coordinator.

The Liberal volunteers try to tie their huge banner to the wire fence but none of the minor party volunteers are willing to move their banners, so they have to go further up the road, and it looks out of place being so far away from the entrance. They move back to the entrance and settle opposite Suzie at the gate while they get organised. Two of them stay with the coordinator, one heads to the main road where the other Labor volunteer is, and an elderly woman holding onto some flyers heads in my direction and parks herself next to me. I get no acknowledgment from her, and she gives the impression she doesn't want to speak to me at all. She's only standing next to me because of the prime position I'm in and she doesn't want me to have any advantage over her. I'm in my blue denim jeans that haven't been washed in a week. The end of my long-sleeved brown chequered shirt hangs out of my jeans, and I have a packet of tobacco sticking out of my breast pocket. I see tinges of light blue in her tightly cropped hair, and her clothes looked like they were just picked up from the dry cleaner. She has white pearls around her neck, glossy red lipstick on her pursed lips and white make-up lightly brushed across her face. I sneak a glance in the million-to-one shot to see if her fingers are nicotine-stained like mine, just to see if we have a skerrick of something in common. She doesn't; we don't.

There is a silence as we wait side by side. The voters come in waves. The next lot ignore me and take Liberal Party pamphlets from the woman. Then a middle-aged woman ignores her and ponies up to me. The next batch, an elderly couple, make a beeline straight to her. I'm watching the elderly couple shuffle away to the entrance as they peruse their pamphlets, when I hear the woman next to me whisper.

'Two–one.'

A woman in her seventies ignores me and chats warmly to the Liberal volunteer. They laugh like they're sisters, they touch arms, they blow kisses, they talk loudly like the only conversation that should be heard is theirs. The old woman is offered a pamphlet but refuses.

'Don't need one, darl,' she says as she heads to the entrance.

I hear the lady whisper again.

'Three–one.'

I turn to face her. She ignores me, then after a few seconds she slowly turns and looks at me.

'Three–one,' she whispers again, hostility laced in her voice. Her eyes pierce mine.

What the fuck's going on, I think. She turns away. I'm invisible again.

A couple my age turn the corner and tread the path towards us. I raise my voice and a chorus of slogans follow.

'Vote Labor, vote Labor, vote Labor.'

'Only John Hewson and the Liberal Party can lead the country forward,' the lady next to me says, just as loudly.

The couple take my pamphlets. They walk away.

I play along.

'Three–all,' I say out of the corner of my mouth.

A middle-aged man approaches us.

'Do you give Paul Keating a head job every morning, you pinko bastard?' the woman whispers to me. The man's only a few steps from us. This well-trimmed lady, who probably lives in Toorak or Prahran, has the mouth of a sewer and has rendered me speechless. The man takes a Liberal Party flyer off the lady, looks at me expectantly, then gives up when I don't offer him one and he walks away. She smiles slyly at me.

'Four–three,' she says. A family of five walk towards us.

She tries to catch me off guard again.

'Do you jack Bob Hawke off, and then wipe his cum on his stomach, you commie poofter!' She makes a vile masturbating motion at me. 'Labor poofter fuckers!'

My jaw may have dropped to the ground once, but it doesn't happen twice.

'Not this time, grandma.'

'Go fuck yourself.'

'Vote Labor, vote Labor, vote Labor.'

'End ten years of misery. Vote Liberal.'

The family of five ignore me and grab the Liberal material from her, then trot away.

' "Vote Labor, vote Labor, vote Labor".' She pouts her lips and mimics me. 'Is that all you have? Six–three to me, you fucking pussy.'

A young couple head towards us.

'Vote Labor. Retain your holiday leave. Keep Medicare. No GST.' They take my flyer, ignore the lady. I look at her.

'Fightback from that, you bitch. Five–six.'

Another run of voters are pooling their way to us.

'You know what my husband and I did after Kerr sacked Whitlam? We fucked by the pool while the neighbours watched. Best fuck of my life. Best day of my life, and we did it again when Fraser won a month later. Suck on that.'

'Lady, I'm going to roll up these flyers and stick them up your fucking …'

'End ten years of Labor power. Vote Keating out. Vote Liberal.' She's caught me off guard again. But I recover, and there is a flurry of hands as flyers are exchanged.

'I won that one. Eight–six to me, you pathetic Labor stooge.'

'Is your husband here? He probably killed himself, just to get away from you, you poisonous …'

'Julian, is everything alright?'

I turn and see Suzie and the Liberal party co-ordinator standing in front of us. We've caused a commotion. Behind them, I see the volunteers from the independent parties watching us from their positions. Our arguments have been loud enough for others to hear and some of them have smirks on their faces. Our theatrics have provided entertainment for the bored volunteers.

'Barbara,' the Liberal coordinator says to her. 'You're making a kerfuffle. You've been warned of this type of behaviour before. Please curb your excitement.'

Barbara sniffs. 'What do you expect, having to put up with this? Look at him. I don't think he's had a shower in a week.' She gestures to me. 'It's insulting.' Her nostrils flare as she turns up her nose. She parries one last time as she scowls at me. 'Intelligence of an ape.'

'She's never been the same since her husband ran away with one of my staffers,' Suzie confides to me in a hushed tone, although the other two can obviously hear it.

'Barbara, we don't stoop to their levels. We're the Liberal Party. We're better than that.'

'What do you mean, Terry?' Suzie interjects. 'You couldn't even get here on time. You lot couldn't run a meat raffle in a pub.'

Terry and Suzie continue their bickering as they walk back to their spots at the gate. The woman and I stand awkwardly next to each other, looking as comfortable as Prince Charles and Lady Diana did during their royal commitments as their marriage was ending.

'You can fuck off with your bullshit about me smelling,' I say to her, breaking the silence. 'While I didn't have time to brush my teeth or comb my hair because I was running late, I'll let you know I showered this morning, not that it's any of your business.'

'Well, you didn't do a very good job, did you? The glue you used last night is still caked over your fingers,' she says to me with smug superiority. 'Idiot.'

I look down at my fingers.

'Oh,' I say.

'Oh, indeed.'

More voters come to us, we hand out flyers, but it's a sedate affair. The abuse and burst of insults have run their course. The voters leave us with flyers of both parties in their hands. We stand together, silent. Then,

'You didn't tell on me?' I ask her.

'Well, where's the fun in that?'

'Did your husband really run away with one of Suzie's helpers?'

Barbara snorts, as if I have no right at all to ask the question, then after a pause she replies in a soft voice.

'He did.'

Another quiet moment passes.

'I'm sorry to hear that.'

'It's okay.'

'This is just boring, now.'

'It is.'

An idea forms.

'There's another polling booth in Lansdowne Street. We can bugger off from here. They've got enough volunteers. There are no coordinators at Lansdowne Street. It's a smaller booth. We can pick a corner and continue our discussions if you like. They'll be no interruptions. What do you say?' I see a tiny hint of acceptance, a tiny smile of anticipation on Barbara's face.

'Okay. I'm in. Let's do it.'

'Great. I need a lift, though. I don't have a car.'

'Oh, for fuck's sake. You're fucking hopeless. Oh

shit. Neither do I. I got a lift with Terry in his car. My car's back at the campaign office.'

'We'll have to catch the bus then.'

'Oh my God, could this day get any worse?'

'Just wait until this evening,' I say to Barbara.

She smiles a second time, a real smile. I see dimples and I know there's warmth and humour somewhere behind her tough exterior. We leave Suzie and the other volunteers, the voters, and the smell of the food cooking, and head away from the school towards the bus stop.

The Bellevue Delmonte

'I don't have the strength anymore. I can't continue. It's a desperate situation. I'm going under.'

It will soon be over. You'll suffer a bit, a couple of minutes at most. I can't lie to you. It will be hard. It's not much compensation, I know.

'Why me? I had so much to live for.'

I know. I'm sorry. Life isn't fair. That's really all I can tell you. You're tired. You've struggled for so long. That's some accomplishment. Others around you have long perished. They're already drifting away from us. I underestimated your strength, your will to live.

'And now it's my turn?'

Yes.

'There's no hand that's going to reach from the sky and lift me from this predicament? There's no almighty saviour to lift me to safety?'

I don't think so. I can't see that happening. I'm truly sorry.

'I pray to God.'

Do that. But do it quickly.

'This suffering you mentioned. Is this it?'

Not even near it. This is paradise compared to what's to follow. Your head is still above water. Just. You're so tired. Every muscle in your body is exhausted. I'm surprised you haven't already gone under. I guess because you're stronger than the other passengers, it bought you more time. When you go under, that's when you'll struggle. I'll be there for you. I promise you that. All the way. I'll help all I can. It's starting to happen now. Water is starting to come into your mouth at the sides. You're too tired to notice. Your legs and arms are nearly still. Once they stop moving, it's time.

'I was so close.'

I know. A butterfly can fly the earth looking for its mate yet be snared in the web of a spider during the final leg of its journey.

'And my journey ends in the bottom of the ocean. How absurd life can be.'

Sorry. Your legs and arms have stopped moving. Have you noticed?

'I can't feel them. Haven't for a while.'

I'm going to ask you to do something for me now.

'Yes?'

You know what it is, don't you?

'Yes. Take some deep breaths.'

Exactly.

'Why bother? It just delays the inevitable.'

You're right. Don't take deep breaths. Just lift your head, look to the sky, open your mouth and let it all come in. You can look at the clouds while the birds hover above you, waiting to pick at your eyes. Oh, you are taking deep breaths after all. Good for you. The instinct to live has kicked in. Fight.

'Then, will it be over?'

No. When you run out of breath, when you have

to open your mouth, that's when the struggle begins. Then it will be over. For now, it's just preservation. But in a way, it's begun. You're under the water. Your cheeks are puffed out. You sucked in every breath you could. You should open your eyes. Have a look around you. Take in the sights.

'You're not being very nice, you know.'

I'm serious. The water is clear, the moon is shining through all the way to the bottom of the ocean. It really is a magnificent sight. All kinds of fish are swimming. Marine life everywhere. Not many people see this, you know. You should think yourself very lucky. Be thankful.

'I'm going to hold my breath for three hours and I'm going to live. I'm going to be pulled from the water. Just to prove you wrong. Then I will punch you.'

Good man. Spite is a powerful force.

'Wait, did you just say I'm lucky? Hang on. Goodness.'

You've opened your eyes. I told you so.

'It is wonderful. There are hundreds of fish around me. The water is teeming with life. Look at all the colours. It's glowing. It's magnificent.'

It is magnificent. Even I'm in awe.

'What are these animals I'm viewing? Some of the fish are blue, others are pink and orange. Some of these animals you can see through, and some change colour. There are shells that have legs, I've never seen anything like it. I feel so insignificant. It's wonderful and sad at the same time. I wish I could hold my breath forever. Can I?'

You can't. When you run out of oxygen, I run out of oxygen. So, I tell myself, I'm going to die if you keep your mouth closed, but if you open your mouth, there's a slight chance, a one in ten million chance, that oxygen instead of water will come flooding in. When I'm out of oxygen, I'll gamble with those odds any day of the week.

'Thanks very much.'

Sorry. Look, let's try and make the most of this situation. It could be worse. You could be in a swirling whirlpool, getting knocked about, things crashing into you. Animals could be sneaking up behind you, taking chunks from you. Enjoy the calmness, the peace.

'You're right. Where are my manners?'

No need for sarcasm.

'Damnation!'

What?

'I see some of the other fellow travellers. Their arms and legs are dangling in front of them. Their hair is drifting in the current. Some of them I recognise. There's a girl, she can't be more than six. They're all dead.'

Sorry you have to see that.

'That will be me in a couple of minutes.'

Sorry.

'Stop saying sorry.'

Sorry.

'I'm running out of breath. It's close. I can't hold on. It's nearly time.'

I know. I can tell. Let it happen. I want you to remember: there are greater things to fear than death.'

'There are? You must tell me more someday. This is where I'm going to thrash about? This is the struggle you've been talking about?'

Yes.

'I'd like to have a good thrash about a bit if you don't mind. My form of protest at my premature demise.'

Thrash all you like. Are you ready?

'I am not.'

Sorry. Here it comes.

'Oh my god. The water's coming down my throat. Oh my god. The brutality.'

I'm sorry.

'This is beastly. It's murder, it is.'

It will be soon over. It's not long now. Think of the good things.

'How can I think of any good things in this predicament?

Listen to me. I want you to think of the one good thing in your life.

'Patricia?'

Correct. Do you remember where you were when you first saw her?

'I do. I was at the market garden, and she was across the field, and she stood out like a rainbow.

I remember walking over towards her, and my legs felt like jelly with each approaching step. When I finally reached her table, I didn't know what to say, and I didn't have any money to buy any of her produce.'

What happened next?

'She sensed that my pockets were empty, but she packed me some fruit and handed it to me, without any expectation that I would pay her. When the top of her fingers brushed against my hand, I shivered. When I looked into her eyes, I saw beauty that I had never seen before. She smiled at me, her skin fair and true, and I fell in love. I tried to say something to her, but I was all tongue-tied.'

I remember. What you said sounded like *hrrrr, gwww, peeww.*

'Yes, my speech was a bit garbled, but we got through it. When I finally asked her name, and she answered 'Patricia', my heart fluttered. When I asked her if she would like to go for a walk in the common after the markets had finished, my life depended on her answer. Luckily she said yes, and I proposed a week later.'

Think of her. Can you do that?

'I've been doing nothing else from the moment I met her. She is golden. She is the sun. If I shovelled a clump of dirt into the palms of her hands, I would explain to her that she is also the earth.'

You are very romantic.

'I have a confession, though. I'm starting to

forget what she's looks like. I'm not thrashing about, anymore, am I?'

You are not.

'I followed my heart and I'm a richer man for the experience. I'm very tired. I'm seeing flashes of white.'

Keep thinking of your beloved. Don't stop.

'I will be thinking of her to the very end. Despite the tragedy that's befallen me, you've made this easier. Thank you.'

My pleasure. Until the next life.

'Until the next life.'

***

'Alright, Simmons, what do we have here?'

'A dead body, sir.'

'Your observations serve you well, Simmons. But I'm more interested in specifics. I'll ask again. What do we have here?'

'Sorry, sir. It's a male body, sir. Cause of death, probable drowning.'

'Why drowning?'

'Because he washed up on the shore, sir.'

'That type of humour might work in theatres in the cities, Simmons, if indeed comedy was the vocation you chose. Am I in a theatre, Simmons? Am I laughing?'

'No, sir.'

'Apply your knowledge and training of science. Deduce, gather, accumulate facts. Yes, probable cause of death is drowning but I want you to study, apply your knowledge, confirm your opinions. He might not have drowned. He could have been killed from a loose piece of wood as the ship went under. He might have fallen, and his chest crushed from a stampede on the deck from the ensuing panic. Look for a cracked skull. Look for broken ribs. Look for anything. Show me what you know, Simmons.'

'Sorry, sir. The body has a tinge of blue from being submerged, sir. There are no signs of decomposition, indicating the body has been in the water for less than forty-eight hours. There is no cracked skull, no broken ribs. There was no loose piece of lumber, no evidence of a stampede on the deck.'

'Good. Continue.'

'The victim was fully clothed at the time of the shipwreck. He was weighed down with his shoes, and with the water in his lungs; his hands have suffered abrasions, an indication, perhaps, of them dragging along the shallow bottom near the shore before the tide washed the body up.'

'Excellent work, Simmons. What else?'

'The body is fresh-smelling. The gases in his body had yet to be released. The body is intact, with minimal exposure to sea creatures, confirming the body hadn't been in the water for too long. Parts of his clothing are torn, an indication the body scraped along rocks as it drifted with the current. If we cut the clothes, I'd expect to find matching cuts and scratches on the body.'

'Good.'

'Thank you, sir. There is seaweed caught in his mouth, his clothes are immersed with sand, and the smell of the sea is overpowering. All observations that point to drowning.'

'Yes, it is an obvious conclusion. We're in a room with other victims who I suspect have suffered the same fate. The victim, Simmons, tell me about him?'

'At a guess, sir, he was yet to reach twenty. The clothes he was wearing, and the rough and ready state of his hands, suggest he was a labourer, or a farmhand of some kind.'

'Anything else?'

'Not really, sir. As this is my third week in your employment, and this is my first encounter with people who have died at sea, and to add, this is the first body from all the bodies here I've examined, I've very little to draw on. I'm feeling a little overwhelmed, to be honest, sir.'

'You've done surprisingly well, Simmons. Maybe I was a bit harsh on you to begin with. My conclusion is the same as yours. The death is due to drowning. The glassy eyes, the colour of the lips are perfect clues. A ship sank at sea and bodies washed up on a shore. We will come to the same conclusions, I imagine, with the autopsies of the others.'

'You have the ship's manifest? You know his name, sir?'

'I do. This man is Jacob Goodman, nineteen years old. This young man followed his fiancée to

Australia. He arrived three months after she did, docked in Brisbane, only to find his betrothed had found gainful employment as a maid in Townsville. He booked a passage to Cairns on the *Bellevue Delmonte,* four days back. The ship foundered during a storm three miles off the Rockhampton coast, sank, and of the thirty-four passengers and crew on board, none survived. Jacob Goodman was from Solihull. Have you heard of Solihull, Simmons? Neither have I. He probably lived in the same village all his life, never travelling a few miles from where he was raised. And his one big adventure, where he follows the love of his life, lands him at the bottom of the Pacific Ocean. Finish the report on this poor man, Simmons, and we'll move on to the other wretched souls. With this heat, their secrets will reveal themselves long before we do. We must hurry up.'

'There was one thing I noticed, sir, but because I'm new to the field, I don't know if I'm imagining it or not.'

'What did you notice?'

'He seems to be smiling, sir. He doesn't look like he is wearing the grimace of upcoming death. He has a grin on his face.'

'Hmmm. You may be right. You have a good eye.'

'I wonder what he was thinking of.'

'We can only ponder. We have to move on, Simmons. We have a long day ahead of us. Come along.'

The queue

The plane landed on time. It rolled down the tarmac and pulled into the terminal. After the harpsichord-looking rubber attachment pieces of the outside stairs had been attached to the plane, the doors were opened and the passengers disembarked through the gate, wheeling their carry-on luggage and holding their phones to their ears as they made their way from the gate.

The queue started to form for the passengers heading for the return flight from Sydney to Brisbane even before the plane had landed. Then when the plane landed the queue snaked from the desk near the gate to outside the lounge, and visitors and arrivals walking to other gates had to sidestep the queue. It comprised families on holidays, couples on a weekend away, FIFO workers, individuals and people on business trips. A normal-looking queue, just like any other queue in any airport in Australia.

A few minutes after the last passenger had exited the plane, an announcement broke over the airwaves:

> Ladies and gentlemen, Jetstar Airlines is pleased to announce that flight JQ410 from Sydney to Brisbane is now ready for boarding through gate number 57. The plane has front and rear entry, so passengers in rows 1 to 16 can use the front entry, and the passengers in rows 17 to 33 can use the staircase at the rear of the plane. Thank you for travelling with Jetstar Airlines.

The pace picked up. Travellers rose from their seats at the gate and joined the long queue. The two female Jetstar crew in their orange uniforms walked from their desk and opened the doors to the plane, then went to the scanning station in front of the doors. The first of the travellers in front of the queue had their boarding passes scanned and started to walk down the ramp to the plane. Slowly, metre by metre, the queue started to move.

Tyler Mariner was at the tail end of the queue; he was kicking his brown leather duffel bag along the ground as the queue shuffled forwards. There was a family in front of him and a pensioner couple behind him. The family were heading to Brisbane to watch an NRL match and were decked out in Roosters colours. They were laughing and chatting amongst themselves. Tyler craned his head over the elderly couple behind him and beyond the end of the queue. The couple held magazines in their hands and Tyler smiled politely at them as he made eye contact. His sixteen-year-old son, Matty, had grabbed fifty dollars off him a couple of minutes before the gate had opened, and disappeared around the corner to the retail shops.

He better hurry up, Tyler thought as the queue gathered pace.

They had flown down to Sydney to visit Tyler's mother for the weekend. Matty had instantly said yes when Tyler asked him if he wanted to come. He thought the reason Matty wanted to come was not to visit his grandmother, but because of the shops that were close by. They lived on the outskirts of Brisbane, and any shops were a drive away, so Matty spent the weekend walking to the shops near his grandmother's house in Sydney to hit the convenience stores and take-away shops. There were plastic wrappers of chocolates and ice cream and empty drink containers that had to be cleaned up from Matty's room when they left. Tyler wasn't too worried. His son exercised at the local gym and didn't eat much junk food at home, so a weekend of Matty piling on the calories was kind of sweet. Despite his teenage posturing and thinking he knew everything, Matty was still a kid.

He's probably just getting one last bag of lollies for the trip, Tyler thought. Matty was over six feet tall, so Tyler just scanned the crowd as he looked for a tall and bored-looking teenager, and soon enough he saw Matty slouching his way towards him amongst the other travellers.

Tyler turned and faced the front. He saw another pair of Jetstar workers, two men in their thirties, move along the side of the queue. One of them was wheeling scales in front of him, and they were weighing the carry-on luggage of the passengers. He knew that Jetstar had a strict policy of weighing carry-on luggage. If your bag weighed over seven kilograms, you were charged fifty bucks. You could still carry your baggage on with you; you didn't have to go to check-in to drop your luggage off, you just needed your credit card on you. A nice little earner for Jetstar, and Tyler watched as the Jetstar staff caught out a couple of unsuspecting travellers. The staff whipped out an iPad, credit cards were swiped and when the credit card transaction was approved the staff wrapped a blue tag around the handles of the luggage, and they wheeled the scales along the queue to the next traveller. Tyler saw that some seasoned travellers in front of him were wearing two sets of tops and extra clothing to keep the weight of their luggage down. They knew the score. Some passengers held heavy books and water bottles in their hands to avoid them going onto the scales, and anything else that might bump up the weight of their luggage and that was small enough was squeezed into their pockets.

When Tyler and Matty had arrived at the airport after his mother had dropped them off, and once they passed through the security screens, Tyler had led them to an empty gate, turned the scales on and weighed their luggage. Both their bags came in at just under seven kilograms. Tyler had emphasised to Matty the need to keep their luggage under seven kilos before their trip to avoid paying any extra fees.

'Yeah, yeah, Dad. Whatever,' his son had replied, shrugging his shoulders, dismissing the advice of his father.

Tyler didn't want to be embarrassed by being picked out for having baggage weighing more than seven kilograms and having the other travellers think he was an idiot. He'd travelled for years on budget airlines, and was well aware of the scams they'd come up with to gouge a little bit more cash from their customers.

There was another reason he didn't want the luggage to be over seven kilograms. Tyler was flat motherless broke. He'd come down to Sydney to ask his mother if he could borrow some money. Business had slowed the last few months and things weren't picking up like they should, so she'd written up a cheque for him. It was nice to catch up with his mother. He tried to see her about four times a year. She lived by herself, was in her eighties, and was excited because she'd just bought two brand new leather recliners, so she and Tyler had spent their time together in front of the telly, enjoying the comfort of the new chairs. They made sure they watched *Murder She Wrote* every night. It was a habit that had crept into his visits. They'd rearrange their routine to make sure they were settled in front of the telly, and just like clockwork, at 5:30, the network played *Murder She Wrote*. The only time they watched the show was when Tyler visited. It was from a bygone era, and Cabot Cove was another world away. Every time he visited, Tyler would pull out his phone and read the shows details. 'Twelve seasons,' he would say to his mother. 'Twelve bloody seasons. 264 episodes. Unbelievable.' His mother would chuckle with him, as she always did, and if they hadn't seen the episode before, they spent the hour trying to guess the murderer. Besides watching old and creaky television shows, they'd go to malls for some shopping, and they'd go to different clubs for dinner and have some wines, and he always had a nice time visiting his mother.

The cheque Tyler's mother had given him was in his wallet, but until it was deposited, it wasn't much use to him. His credit card was maxed out, and Matty had just grabbed the last of his cash and wandered off for a bit of last-minute shopping. Tyler was so broke he didn't even know if there was enough money on their Go Cards to catch the bus from Brisbane airport to get home.

Matty shuffled up to him and joined him in the queue, shimmied his backpack off his shoulders and placed it next to Tyler's duffel bag on the floor. The queue moved forward; the Jetstar workers moved forward as well, and were weighing the luggage of the travellers, wrapping tags around the handles, charging travellers whose baggage was over seven kilograms, and they were slowly making their way to Tyler and Matty. Tyler glanced down to Matty's backpack.

'What the fuck!'

Sticking out of Matty's backpack was a Lego box. A big yellow Lego box. Matty couldn't zip his backpack up because the Lego box he'd just bought wouldn't fit in his bag.

'What the fuck, Matty?' Tyler repeated, almost yelling. The Jetstar staff were slowly making their way down the queue, weighing all the carry-on luggage. There was no question about it. The hundreds of tiny pieces in the Lego box, even though they weighed only a few hundred grams, would tip Matty's luggage over the seven-kilogram limit.

'There's no way that will fit in your bag or mine,' Tyler said in shock to his son. 'That looks expensive, too.'

'It wasn't. It was on special.'

'Good. Do I at least get any change back?'

'No.'

'Why not?'

'Because I bought this as well.'

In Matty's other hand he produced a big tub of protein powder. Tyler's eyes widened with rage and fear as he read the label. The tub weighed three kilograms.

'Fuck!'

'It's cheaper than the one I normally buy, Dad.'

Tyler felt his veins popping out of his head. Other travellers looked Tyler's way to see what the commotion was. They smirked when they saw what was happening. They understood the situation Tyler was in. The Jetstar workers and the scales were only metres away. The travellers in front of him going to the rugby league were taking off their shoulder bags and picking up their carry-on luggage, waiting for the scales to roll up to them. Tyler was going to get pinged for excess carry-on luggage, and he didn't have any cash on him, nor on his credit card to pay for it.

'Oh, my god, Matty, they won't fit in any of the bags. How are we going to get them on the plane?'

Matty shrugged.

'Dunno.'

Tyler didn't know what to do. He bent down and opened his duffel bag. There was no spare room for a box of Lego, let alone a bucket of protein powder. The family in front of him were loading their bags onto the scales. He zipped his bag back up and grabbed the Lego sticking out of Matty's bag. An idea popped into his head. It was all he could think of.

'Stick that protein tub up your jumper,' Tyler hurriedly said to his son as he tucked the Lego box up his tee-shirt.

'What?' Matty asked.

'Don't argue with me, son, just stick it up your fucken jumper.'

Matty reluctantly shoved the tub of protein powder up his jumper just as the Jetstar staff arrived with the scales. Tyler had a square-shaped box of Lego sticking out of his tee-shirt in front of his stomach, and Matty had his tub of protein powder sticking out of him like he was hiding a termite mound

'Sir,' the Jetstar attendant said to him, 'can you please place your luggage on the scales for …'

The attendant stopped mid-sentence. He saw the box protruding from Tyler's stomach, then he saw Matty with his big tub of powder bulging out from under his jumper. Tyler silently placed their two bags on the scales, then stared blankly ahead as he stood in the queue next to his son. The weight of the two bags was just under fourteen kilograms, but the attendant was too preoccupied to notice. His mouth was as open as a fish at feeding time. He nudged his co-worker with his elbow.

'You seeing this, Pete?'

Pete looked at Tyler, then at Matty and then at their bulging garments.

With a weary smile on his face, Pete ripped two blue tags off the handle of the scales and wrapped them around the handles of the two bags.

'Nothing to see here,' he replied as he wheeled the scales along the queue to the next lot of travellers.

Shadows and tall trees

The doctor I saw was having none of it. He'd seen grifters like me many times, pleading their malaise, their illness, then at the end of the consultation ask for a certificate for time off work. Even if in my case, asking for a medical certificate was justified. The doctor had summoned me into his office a few minutes after I'd checked in, then rapped his thick stubby fingers on his desk as I told him of my recent woes. My hopes for a certificate were diving with each rap of his knuckles.

Because I'd recently moved interstate, I hadn't settled on a regular doctor, so with my recent illness, I'd been chasing any appointment with any general practitioner I could find. As soon as I'd moved, my heart started playing up, I was hospitalised, and I'd been having long stints off work, and I needed certificates so I could continue to get paid. Most of the doctors were accommodating. Once I mentioned my recently diagnosed heart issues, they couldn't write a certificate for me quick enough. But the doctor I was sitting in front of now, Dr Hardcastle, had his head down as he listened to me ramble on about my headaches and tingling toes and fingers, then finish by asking for the next seven days off work and the accompanying certificates that went with it – I could tell I was going to have difficulties. He wouldn't look me in the eye. I was talking to the top of his curly head as he stared down at his desk and his curly head was shaking before I'd finished.

Once I stopped speaking, he lifted his head, screwed up his face and looked at me with weary ash-coloured eyes.

'Nope,' he said to my request.

He cut me off before I went to plan B, which was just as well, because there was no plan B. He went on his computer and his thick fingers clacked away as he checked my history.

'Gerry,' he began. 'The heart condition you have is common. You shouldn't be having all this time off work because of it. The x-rays you had show your arteries are fine. And with the medication you're taking, you shouldn't be getting headaches.'

Dr Hardcastle then proceeded to give me a thorough examination. I stripped down to my singlet and boxers. I was weighed, my height measured, my blood pressure checked. He listened to my heart with his stethoscope.

'Nothing wrong with it,' he muttered to himself.

I lifted my tongue and went 'agggh' when he stuck a popsicle stick in the bottom of my mouth. Then he directed me back to the chair by the desk.

'Gerry,' Dr Hardcastle said when he sat back down. He reached for his pen. 'Is there any history of diabetes running in the family?'

'No.'

'Hypertension?'

'No.'

'Any common cancers running in the family?'

'No.'

'Do you sleep well?'

'No.'

'Any mental illness in the family?'

'Yes.'

'Any thoughts of suicide?'

'Um, doesn't everyone?'

I walked out of his office five minutes later with a certificate for three days instead of seven and, as a bonus, a diagnosis of depression. As I waited in line at reception to pay the doctor's invoice, I read over the anti-depressant he'd prescribed me. Paroxetine. Never heard of it.

An uncle had committed suicide when I was younger; with life in general, I'd been melancholic myself for most of my thirties and forties. Now I was in my fifties, melancholy was as dominant as the blood that ran through my veins. When I'd see people laugh or smile, if I had passed them on the street or overheard jovial conversations around me, I was jealous, and had been for years. The added diagnosis of depression was unexpected, but no surprise.

The line in front of me thinned, and the receptionist waved me over. I had asked the doctor as he handed me the script, when I was getting ready to leave, how I'd feel once I started taking the drug.

'Normal,' he had told me.

I swiped my card at the machine, and the receipt started to print out on a nearby desk.

Normal? I thought. What the fuck does that even mean?

***

My son, Raphael, was hiding behind the door of his bedroom when I arrived home. I'd thrown the keys on the bench by the front door and was halfway down the hallway when he snuck up on me from behind and punched me three times, sharp and hard, on my arm.

'Pinch and a punch, start of the month,' my seventeen-year-old son said with a wide grin on his face.

We'd been playing the game since before he was a teenager, and every month I forgot about it until I saw his fast-approaching form barrelling towards me. I winced in pain. Raphael, my only child, was taller than me, had arms thicker than an axeman's, and had more muscles than I had wrinkles. Could he remember to do his homework, make his bed or clean his room? Of course not. Could he remember at the start of every month to sneak up on me and bruise my arm? My tender and aching arm for the first week of each month were proof that for years, he could.

'Ouch, you bugger,' I said as I rubbed my arm. 'You got me again. You're just lucky, you punk.' The script I'd picked up from the chemist spilled from its paper wrapper when he pounded my arm. Raphael bent down, picked it up and regarded it closely.

'What's this, old man loser?' he asked.

'Old man happy pills,' I answered, not really knowing how to respond. Raphael pulled his phone from his pocket, took a picture of the packet.

'Hmmmm,' he said. Then he handed my script back to me and went to his room.

I went to the kitchen and warmed up last night's dinner, then messaged my boss, telling him of my diagnosis, and that I wouldn't be in for another week. With only receiving a certificate for three days, I would have to use some of my annual leave.

His one-word text came when I was getting ready for bed a couple of hours later: Okay.

Every night when I went to bed, I left the edge of the curtains slightly ajar, which enabled me to look out my window as I lay on my pillows to the tops of my neighbour's trees across the road. I would watch the leaves and branches of the trees sway in the breeze. That night I heard cats prowling in the courtyard below and music from a party two floors up was playing. My phone pinged. Another message. Raphael.

Dad, can I get my learners? Can I learn to drive?

Of course you can. What do I have to do?

Not much. I just need my birth certificate, my passport. I can do everything else.

Okay.

With Raphael's consistently high marks at school, he was destined for bigger things: going to university was a no-brainer. There was no university in the town we'd moved to, so we both knew this year would be our last of us living together. We'd talked about it. He'd rent a room on the campus at the university he was going to apply for. I'd been putting away money for it; he'd found part-time work at a café in town, and was squirrelling his cash away as well.

The music two floors up was louder, matched by the shrieks of the revellers. I was going to miss Raphael when he moved, even though he spent most of his time in his bedroom, and we hardly saw each other when we were home. When we were in the same room, having dinner, or on a bus, cramped together, we didn't speak much. But we didn't need to. The silence we shared was comfortable enough. Teaching him to drive would be a nice way of spending our last year together before he moved.

I concentrated my gaze on the swaying trees across the road, and they made me forget about the noise of the cats below and the party above. The trees lulled and soothed me, and I slowly fell asleep.

***

You got your learners? Good on you.

When can we go for a lesson? I need 120 hours before I can go for my licence.

Tomorrow if you like. After work.

Okay.

***

'You're on the wrong side of the road.'

'No, I'm not. You're on the wrong side of the road.'

'What a stupid thing to say. And slow down. You're going too fast.'

'No, I'm not.'

'How many hours is it again to get your licence?'

'One hundred and twenty.'

'Fuck.'

***

'How are you feeling, Gerry?'

'The same. Felt sleepy for the first couple of days, but no change.'

'We can up the dosage if you want. We have plenty of options.'

'Okay. Maybe up the dosage.'

'I can give you time off work if you like, while you adjust to the different medication.'

'You can? That's great.'

'Just a couple of days. What did you think I'd give you? A month or something?'

'A couple of days is fine. Thanks.'

***

I was in the loungeroom, reading, when I heard a knock at the front door.

'Telegram for Mr Kinnear,' a voice said. 'Telegram for Mr Kinnear.'

I walked down the hallway, past Raphael's bedroom, and opened the front door.

There was a portable tape deck sitting on top of the door mat. 'Telegram for Mr Kinnear,' the tinny voice coming from the tape recorder repeated. I turned but was too late. He knocked me so far, I had to hang onto the stairwell railing to keep myself from falling down the stairs.

'Telegrams haven't existed since you were a kid, old man, but you still fell for it.' Raphael chuckled, then returned to his bedroom.

The following month I went back to my bedroom after breakfast to make the bed, when I saw a pair of shoes sticking out from under the curtains. 'It's that time of the month, hey,' I thought. I tiptoed to the windows, and with a flourish pulled the curtains back with my fist ready, thinking I'd got him this time, but there was nothing there but the pair of shoes. He snuck up on me from behind and pounded my arm so hard I bounced off the window pane.

'Didn't you even realise they were your shoes? You're such an idiot.'

'Shaddup.'

***

'You're too close to the gutter. Get into the middle of the road a bit more.'

'I'm fine.'

'You're speeding, too.'

'No, I'm not. Why do you keep reaching for the door handle?'

'No reason. How many hours left?'

'Ninety-five. Why?'

'The hours are just flying by, aren't they, mate? Watch out for that pedestrian, Raphael.'

'The one on the footpath?'

'Yep.'

'Be quiet.'

***

I was on the balcony having a cup of tea, reading the paper, enjoying the morning sun. I didn't hear the door slide open, and I didn't hear him sneak up on me. I just felt his lurking presence from behind. I turned and he was towering over me, his fist already clenched, his face joyful with anticipation.

'Is it the first of the month already?'

'It is.'

'Can I at least put down my cup of tea?'

'No.'

My tea spilt onto the concrete; the saucer smashed onto the ground. He disappeared back into the flat, and a minute later, as I was cleaning up, the door slid back open, and the car keys were thrown onto the table. Five minutes later, we were on the road.

The hours in his logbook filled up over the months. Every weeknight, and on the weekends, we'd be in the car. We drove around the town, on the outskirts, to and from his work for his shifts. His driving was fine. Like everything else he attempted, he seemed to be a natural. His reverse parking was much better than mine. For every hour of a lesson he had with an instructor, he was credited with three. He would soon get to 120 hours and the driving lessons we shared would soon come to a halt. So would his time living with me. I tried not to think about it.

***

'How you been going, Gerry?'

'Not bad, Doctor. I remember you telling me when you first diagnosed me with depression that after I started taking the pills, that I'd feel normal. I have to confess, I have no idea what being normal means.'

Dr Hardcastle laughed.

'Did I say that? Sorry. That was a throwaway line. I don't know what normal means, either.'

'Well, I had come in begging for a certificate the first time I'd seen you. You didn't know me.'

'I know. I was worried about you. Are your toes and fingers still tingling? Are you still getting headaches?'

'Now that you mention it, I haven't had either for some time.'

'Good. You mentioned your son is moving in the new year?'

'He will be. His teachers have told me he's one of the smartest in school and he should be able to pick and choose where he wants to go. There's no university in this town, so he'll be off.'

'That will be tough for you. Be prepared.'

'I'm dreading it when he leaves. I might need some time off as I adjust to living on my own, Doctor.

What's it called? Empty nest syndrome? Any self-respecting doctor would give me some leave for that, surely?'

Dr Hardcastle laughed. 'Nice try, Gerry.'

For the first time, I left his office smiling.

Winter ended, and the months became warmer. The school year was drawing to an end and Raphael was busy with his exams. There were textbooks and papers strewn across the lounge room. I heard him more than I saw him. His swearing from his bedroom echoed throughout the flat as he struggled with some of his studies. I left him to it.

I'd bought some cat food on my way home from work one afternoon. I was sitting on the front steps at the entrance of the unit complex and was feeding the tabbies that roamed the courtyard. I petted them gently as they crawled around my legs, purring after they'd finished their meal. I still didn't know what normal was but feeding and petting stray cats and receiving affection from them seemed a normal thing to do.

One of my neighbours, a man in his twenties, one of the party-goers who lived in the flat two floors above, brushed past me and disappeared up the stairwell carrying a bag of shopping. He nodded to me then was on his way. I thought about having a talk to him about his music, but then thought, it could wait. I'd speak to him later. The music didn't bother me as much as it used to a few months back. Maybe the anti-depressants I was taking were working after all.

I was watching the cats prowl around the courtyard when I heard a jingle of keys ring in my ears a couple of minutes later. It was Raphael.

'Shouldn't you be studying?' I asked him.

'Nuh,' he replied. 'I'm just about done. Let's do some driving.' He punched me in the arm. My arm felt like it had been riddled with bullets.

'Shit. It's the beginning of the month, is it?'

'It's the first of November, Dad. You're such a dumbass. Let's go.'

We finished clocking up his driving hours midway through November. Raphael passed his driving test at his first attempt. My phone pinged when I was at work. His driving instructor had taken a picture of him in front of his car as Raphael proudly held a 'P' plate in his hand.

His school marks were so high he was offered placements at universities across the country. Raphael accepted a spot at the university in the nearest town. I breathed a sigh of relief. I'd been crossing my fingers as he mulled over which university to choose.

I ticked off the days until the start of December. I tried to sneak up on him, have one win, but he beat me to it. My alarm went off at 6, but his must have gone off at 5:55am. I saw movement in the dark, a silent figure in pyjamas skulking in the hallway when I opened my bedroom door. A few seconds later I was leaning against the linen cupboard in the hallway, grimacing in pain.

'Merry Christmas, hopeless old man,' he said, before he headed to the kitchen pantry to make his breakfast.

My Christmas bonus from work was larger than usual. I told Raphael I was transferring something big into his account and to let me know when it came through. With a big grin on my face, I transferred five dollars into his account.

Many thanks. I think.

Revenge for sore arms.

The next morning, I transferred two thousand dollars to his account.

Thanks, dad.

No worries.

We spent the Christmas break packing up his things for his move. We spent the new year long weekend at a motel near his university after we'd spent the day at his campus, moving his gear into the room he was renting, checking out the facilities, then spending the evening exploring the town.

I thought I was ready for him on New Year's Day. I woke up early in the motel room we were sharing. The crumpled figure of Raphael was still sleeping in his bed. I went over to the bed with my arm raised and my knuckles ready and pulled back the sheets. I didn't see Raphael; I saw pillows and rolled-up blankets instead. I heard footsteps from behind coming from the bathroom, I turned and raised my fist, but was too slow. My first waking moments of the new year were spent nursing an aching arm.

Raphael moved out in the middle of January. I hugged him so tightly at the front door I heard him sigh and groan. I didn't care. In the end he had to pull himself away from me. He had a train to catch, but I was too upset to accompany him to the station, so I stood at the front door of the flat as I heard his footsteps echo on the stairs down to the ground floor. I went to the balcony and saw him walk through the courtyard, then he turned and saw me watching him like he knew I would be. He waved, smiled, turned the corner and was gone. I looked to the trees across the road I watched to help me sleep at night. They were swaying with the morning breeze. They seemed to be saying to me, *It will be okay, Gerry. He's a great kid. You did a wonderful job. He'll be right.* That imagined reassurance failed to halt a well of tears falling down my cheeks.

That night the party-goers two floors up were partying hard. The music was pounding through my walls. Even with the medication I was taking, my tolerance had come to an end. I reached for my phone and rang the unit supervisor.

'Doug,' I said to him when he picked up. 'Those pricks on the sixth floor are having one of their parties again. I'm a bit over it, mate.'

'They are?' Doug replied. 'I've had so many complaints about them. Those buggers are on their third and final warning. Leave it with me.'

Ten minutes later the music stopped, and the complex was quiet. Lying in bed, I stared through my window at the tops of the trees as the wind blew through the leaves and the branches, but all I saw was the image of Raphael as he walked down the steps and away from me earlier in the day. It was a long night.

It was a long few days. The house was so empty after he left. I missed him so much. I sat on his bed and sniffed his pillows, and my tears spilled onto his sheets. Around the house I wore his jeans and tops, and I opened the pantry and fridge doors just to be reminded of the sounds he made when he was home. I even wished the party-goers would crank out their music, just for the distraction. I was so listless at work I made mistakes, and wasn't overly fussed to fix them. Opening the front door of your house when you came home, knowing it would be empty, and would always be empty, was a gut-wrenching experience that was going to take time to get used to.

***

'Gerry, you look well. Haven't seen you for a while. How are you?'

'My boy's gone, Doctor. Fuck.'

'I know, mate. My two flew the coop years back. It takes time to adjust. My advice, don't do anything rash or sudden for six months.'

'That's alright. I'm too busy crying into my box of tissues to do anything anyway. Do you have some empty-nester sedatives you can prescribe for me? Jumbo size, maybe?'

Doctor Hardcastle laughed.

'Funny man. How have you been, really, Gerry?

'Actually, besides Raphael leaving, not too bad.'

'Good. I can reduce your dosage if you like. Gradually get you off them.'

'Sounds good.'

I booked a week off work from the end of January, and on the Monday, I caught a train to visit Raphael. We'd been in constant contact since he left. He'd settled in at university, was thriving. He'd also found a part-time job at a café on campus, made new friends. I felt regretful and guilty about my selfishness in my reluctance to let him go. Having a child leave was a natural part of parenthood. Who was I to get in his way? When the train pulled into the platform, I jumped out and walked to the taxi rank, stepped into the back of the cab, and asked to be taken to the university.

I had a plan. I knew Raphael was rostered on at the café, but he didn't know I was coming, and I was surprising him with this visit. I was going to walk into the café, walk past the counter. It was the first day of February after all. There was a shock coming for Raphael. I was going to head into the kitchen, sneak up behind him and bop him right on the arm. *'Take that!'* My moment of triumph would almost trump the humiliation he was going to suffer in front of his co-workers.

I walked into the café, but things didn't go as planned. The young waitress, instead of directing me to a table, came up to me and lightly punched me on the shoulder.

'You're expected, Mr Kinnear,' she said with a big cheeky grin on her face.

The barista, a muscled hipster-looking fellow in a tight striped tee-shirt with a fancy moustache, stopped making his coffees, walked from his machine at the side of the café and punched me on the arm.

'Pleased to meet you, Gerry. I'm Ronny.' His smile was as wide as the waitress's.

And there he was. I saw Raphael at the back of the kitchen with his back to me. He towered over the sink as he washed the dishes. He was dressed in black jeans, a white shirt, scuffed runners and yellow gloves as he put a freshly washed saucepan on the drying rack. I walked past the counter, dropped my suitcase by my feet and tapped him on the shoulder.

'I thought I had you this time.'

'You'll never have me, old man,' he said as he faced me. 'You're as predictable as the morning sun.'

He peeled his gloves off and we hugged. I hugged him longer than I had ever hugged him and I squeezed him tighter than I'd ever squeezed him. He was so tall his chin rested on the top of my head. I must have looked a fool, but I didn't care. I loved him more than life, had been miserable since he left, and was overjoyed to now be with him. I realised that the emotions that overwhelmed me were normal emotions. He pulled away from our embrace, smiling. I knew he was going to be okay.

I was going to be okay.

How to kill a rooster

David Mackay and his wife, Angela, bought a house, finally. After years of saving and scrimping, working every minute of overtime, putting off holidays, buying clothes at op shops, and staying home instead of going to restaurants, they did it. David Mackay did everything he could, from banking coins he kept in jars, to putting their annual tax returns towards the deposit. He had spreadsheets on his computer that he looked at all the time to help them reach their goal. He set up separate accounts to hide their savings, so as not to be tempted, and he ticked off his savings plan on his spreadsheet each fortnight. He remained positive despite being priced out of suburb after suburb as prices ballooned across the city. When they first started looking, he and Angela went to an auction in the inner-city suburb where they lived, just to get an idea of what they might be facing. They stood amongst the crowd, their fingers tightly clenched around their coffee cups, aghast, in disbelief and dismay, as the price of the one-bedroom flat on the bottom floor in an ugly block of units on a busy street kept going up and up and sold for a price that was way above their expectations. David's shoulders slumped as he realised what they had saved up was never going to be enough for a deposit in the area they wanted to live. David realised he would have to kiss goodbye to the cafés, pubs and the inner-city life he enjoyed so much. He remained positive though, as they widened their search to areas further out of town and drove around the western suburbs. Angela sat in the passenger seat in stony silence as they drove past fibro and red-brick houses. David realised he couldn't even afford houses in some of the suburbs they were driving through, even though they were forty kilometres from the city. When they arrived back to their flat, Angela was nearly in tears.

'I love you, David, but if you're moving to the western suburbs, you'll be moving on your own,' she told him.

He was glad she had told him that. He couldn't do it either. The western suburbs were a different world. Vast, never-ending, stifling hot in summer, and he couldn't comprehend why anyone would choose to live there. But David had realised, as he had driven past rows and rows of the same soulless houses, units and townhouses, that the residents of the western suburbs had over the years made the same decision David was facing up to now. They couldn't afford to live near the city either.

He widened his search even further and looked online at what was for sale in the mountains west of the city. He found houses that they could afford, but it was so far from where they worked. It was an uneasy equation to grapple with. Commuting five days a week to work and back, navigating the bumper-to-bumper peak-hour traffic. It would be grinding and numbing. In the end though, both he and Angela realised if they wanted to buy a house that was the sacrifice they would have to make.

So the next weekend they headed up the mountains. They met a real estate agent at her office as they had made appointments to view three houses. The first house was on a hill with a water tower on the other side of the road. It was a small house with caravan ply for walls in the rooms. The second house they looked at was a bit confronting. As soon as you opened the door, you were already in the lounge room. The walls were dirty and some of the rooms were still being renovated. The third house was a weatherboard cottage at the bottom of a hill in a street off the highway. It was just as run down as the other two houses, but they both got a good feeling as they walked around the rooms. They saw more positives than negatives. They wanted to start a family and the house was big enough. There were three bedrooms, the front verandah had been enclosed, and there was a large chimney that had a wood heater in the lounge room and in the kitchen. The paint on the walls was bright and colourful, and the afternoon sun shone through. The floorboards were crooked and sloped at different angles in the original rooms of the house, but the kitchen windows looked out onto the street and gave them wonderful views of trees and other houses. There were gardens in the backyard that were overgrown; tall hedges instead of fences that ran along both sides of the house gave the house extra privacy. There was a garage in front of the driveway, a separate laundry outside and two paths lined with pebbles that led from the front gate to the front door and up the side of the house. The best bit was, after years of saving for a house close to the city, they could slap down a deposit if they wanted to and they could easily afford the repayments of a house a hundred kilometres out of town.

They were excited on the way back home. They couldn't stop talking about the last house they saw. Despite its imperfections, to them the house was perfect.

'Should we make an offer?' Angela asked David.

'That's what I was thinking,' David replied.

'Should we look at more houses? I mean, this is our first time we've even looked up here.'

'But I'm happy with that last house we looked at.'

'So am I.'

The next morning David rang the real estate agent. He tried his luck and offered thirty thousand dollars less than the asking price. The agent rang him back ten minutes later and said, 'Nooo.' He then offered the asking price. The agent rang back in ten minutes time and said, 'Congratulations, the house is yours.'

In the lead-up to moving in, they drew plans of changes they were going to make. There were definitely some things that needed to be fixed. They wanted to rip up the carpet in the sunroom and the back bedrooms. It was white and frayed and showed up all the dust and dirt that fell to the floor. The roof of the laundry leaked, and the concrete floor in the garage was old and crumbling. Angela had sketched designs for a garden; they wanted a pergola built in the backyard. An apple tree was too close to the back door and David thought the apples would clog the gutters when they fell from the tree, so he wanted to chop it down. He'd lived all in his life in flats. He looked forward to buying tools and creating things for the house.

There were no problems with the exchange. Everything went smoothly. A representative from their bank came to their flat and gave final approval for the loan. They pre-signed all the documents their solicitor sent to them, put them in the post and after a few weeks of not hearing anything their solicitor rang them on a Friday to let them know settlement was going ahead. A week later he rang again. 'All done,' the solicitor said. 'It's officially yours. Congratulations.' A run-of-the-mill sale for the solicitor was heaven for David and Angela. They went to the pub that night to have a few celebratory ales. In the run-up to moving they had garage sales in the carport of their complex to get rid of stuff they didn't want. They caught up with residents in the block they rarely saw.

Before they moved, David drove to the new house three times, all at night. He went twice on a Saturday night, and once during a weeknight. It was over an hour and a half away, so each time he told

Angela he was going to visit his mate for a while. He didn't like lying to her, but he didn't want her to know what he was up to. He had phobias he didn't want her to know about.

He'd never liked living in units, even though he'd done so all his life. It was suffocating having people living above and below him. He didn't like hearing conversations of other residents through the walls, taps in someone else's kitchens being turned on and off, or smelling someone else's cooking. It had never been for him. He couldn't wait until he moved to a house.

So David drove the ninety minutes by himself to the house they were buying in the mountains. On the first occasion, it was dark and blowing a gale when he pulled up on the other side of the road. There was a 'sold' sign on the advertising board on the nature strip in front of the house. His chest swelled with pride: the hundred-year-old weatherboard cottage was soon to be his and Angela's home. There were lights on inside and he saw people moving about, but he had no desire to meet the owners. He had driven up to see if the neighbourhood had any nasty surprises in store when they moved in. Like dogs that barked, or a party house that played music all night, or teenagers that ran amok. He had checked the Airbnb website to see if there were any holiday houses in the area. But each time David walked up and down the street on his three trips, pricking up his ears, he heard nothing. He did hear the leaves from trees blowing in the strong breeze, and the train from up near the highway hurtling through town, but that was it. He saw a cat dart across the road, kids' bikes lying on their sides in front yards. It seemed a quiet neighbourhood. No loud music, no barking dogs, no holiday houses. Even though each time he visited he stayed no longer than fifteen minutes – a tiny microcosm of time to gauge whether it was a quiet area – he was satisfied. They had made the right choice. There wasn't much more he could do.

They rented the biggest truck they could hire that only required a driver's licence and moved themselves up the mountains to their new home. They were lucky. Their employers had granted both of them annual leave, so they had a month off together to settle into their new house. They hadn't sold as much of their belongings as they thought they would, so it took them three trips to move everything up. On the first trip they stopped at the real estate agency in the village and picked up the keys. They parked the truck on the nature strip and ran up the path to the stairs. Their hands were shaking as together they inserted the key in the lock of the front door. Then they both turned the key. The door opened. David followed Angela as she walked into the sunroom. They shrieked with joy. Their first steps in their new house.

They spent the day driving up and down the highway, loading and unloading the van, only staying a short time at their new house to drop their stuff off quickly so they could go back down the highway for another load. By the time they were finished there was a couch and a television in their lounge room, a fridge in the kitchen and a mattress in the bedroom. There were boxes all over the place. They made one last trip down the highway to drop off the truck. The rental shop was closed so they left the truck in the parking lot and the keys in a slot in the front door, then drove their own cars back up the highway to their new place.

They ordered pizza and had dinner on the couch. David went outside in the dark and picked up pieces of kindling on the ground and they had their first dinner and wine in their new place sitting on their couch in front of a fire. It was the first time David had ever lit a fire. He had bought some fire starters just for the occasion. The glass of the wood heater glowed as the fire kicked in and heated the room. Angela and David were exhausted. Earlier on during the day they had both been talking about going to the local pub to have some drinks but spending the whole day moving had taken its toll. They were done. Their bones were aching, and they could hardly move. They hadn't assembled their bed, so they carelessly threw some sheets and blankets on the mattress that was lying on the floor and slumped onto it just after nine pm. Five minutes after drawing the blankets over themselves, they were fast asleep.

***

David was dreaming of when he was younger, and he was hanging out with his dad. He was about five or six. His father was teaching him how to ride a pushbike and was holding him up from behind as the bike wobbled and David struggled to gain control of it. He could hear his father's running footsteps pounding behind him as he put his feet on the pedals and became more confident. He gathered speed and then he could hear his father's footsteps slowly receding as he rode away from his father. His father started cheering. But his father's cheers were replaced with another noise.

Cock-a-doodle-do.

Cock-a-doodle-do.

Cock-a-doodle-do.

David woke from his dream, confused and sleepy. He rubbed his eyes and checked his phone. It was 4:30 in the morning. What was going on? Then he heard it again.

Cock-a-doodle-do.

He sat up, and for an instant he forgot where he was. Then he remembered. It was the first night in their new house and he was dreaming about his dad teaching him how to ride a bike and he was woken at 4:30 by … what was it? A noise from outside.

Cock-a-doodle-do.

'What the fuck is that?' David thought. He got out of bed and walked down the back hallway and opened the back door. It was dark outside, but the noise came again, louder and clearer this time.

Cock-a-doodle-do.

'No fucking way,' David thought as his stomach filled with dread. 'Don't tell me we're living next door to someone who has a rooster. Fuck me dead.'

Then he heard Angela sleepily yell out from the bedroom, 'What the fuck!' It had woken her up too.

They stood in the kitchen a few minutes later, nursing their morning cups of coffee. In the still and quiet of the morning darkness, they heard it again and again and again.

Cock-a-doodle-do.

'This isn't good,' Angela said, still half asleep as she put the kettle on for another coffee.

'No, it isn't.' David had by then already ducked to all corners of their house. He could hear the rooster crowing in every room. It was so loud it was like it was living under their house. But it was the noisiest in their bedroom. When morning came, they stood outside and realised the rooster belonged to their neighbour on the right. They must keep chickens, and they must have a rooster as well. The coop must have been situated near the hedge on the neighbour's side. They couldn't see the chickens, the coop or the rooster because of the thick hedge, but they could hear the gentle cluck of the chickens every now and again.

Bok bok, bok.

Bok bok, boookkk.

And of course, a rooster living with the chickens.

Cock-a-doodle-do.

David and Angela found out that roosters don't crow just at the beginning of sun-up. They crow all day. Angela went online and did a bit of research. One article claimed they crow on average fifteen times a day. Angela scoffed. 'More like fifteen times a minute.' When they were unpacking later in the morning, on what should have been the best day of their lives, as they rearranged furniture and filled the shelves and cabinets with belongings and hooked up the telly, all they could hear was the crowing of the neighbour's rooster.

David was kicking himself. He hadn't thought of a rooster at all when he scouted the neighbourhood searching for any distracting noises. Why would he? He didn't even think roosters were allowed in residential areas anymore anyway. When the rooster woke them up the next morning at 4:35, David turned on his side, grimacing and cursing. Were you allowed to keep roosters at all, he wondered? Surely not. As the rooster crowed again, this time waking Angela up, he determined to find out.

David was wrong. He'd thought the problem would be fixed with a simple phone call. He rang his local council and spoke to a Sally Anne. Sally Anne was very polite and apologetic as David explained their situation but, in the end, not helpful. Where they lived in the mountains was classed as semi-rural, so you could keep as many chickens and roosters as you or your neighbour liked. 'But it's five metres away from our house,' David protested futilely. He hung up the phone. He couldn't believe it. David turned to Angela, who was standing next to him, listening in on the conversation.

'We're fucked ten times until Sunday,' he said to her as he put the phone down.

'Oh no,' Angela said. Even as David was talking to the council lady, he could hear the rooster crowing in the background. This was not a good situation at all.

'How come we didn't hear it when we looked at the house?'

'I have a theory. The previous owner was probably in cahoots with the neighbour. They must have moved it or something whenever there was an inspection. Who'd buy a house with a rooster crowing in their ear?'

'What do we do?' Angela asked.

David put his arms around his wife to comfort her. 'I don't know. Maybe we'll get used to it,' he replied in a not very hopeful tone.

They moved their mattress to the room furthest away from the house with the rooster. They shut all the doors at night to muffle the noise. It didn't work. They were both woken up by its crowing at 4:39 am.

'Davey, baby, you have to do something. This is ridiculous,' Angela groggily said to him at 4:41.

'Okay, anything for you. There's only one thing left to do.'

'What's that, honey?'

'Eat it.'

'Okay, baby. Just be careful.' Angela went back to sleep for another three minutes until the rooster woke her up again at 4:46.

'If you don't do it, I will,' she said, as she put a pillow over her head and tried to get back to sleep.

They still had over three weeks of holidays left. David wanted it sorted by the time they went back to work. He didn't want to be thinking about it as he drove up and down the highway to work every day. He didn't want to knock on the neighbour's door and complain about it. If council said roosters were okay, there wasn't much he could do. If he did complain to the neighbours and they were a bit narky, they might get another rooster just to piss David off even more. So, he had to be a bit clever about it. He didn't want to draw attention to himself, so he'd have to have a good plan. All the work they wanted to do on the house would be put on the backburner. This was a priority. As he lay in bed, unable to get back to sleep because of the crowing of his neighbour's rooster, he thought of a plan.

He had to know what he was dealing with first, so in the morning he went to the electronics shop and bought a drone. He charged the battery, set up the bluetooth and sent it over to his neighbour's backyard.

The footage was relayed to his phone. The coop was long, wooden and rectangular with thick wiring, and ran along the thick hedge that bordered the two houses. There was a gate at the front, and a small shed for the chickens to sleep in during the night. There were wood shavings on the floor with feeding tins and troughs. There was a tin roof over the shed and more wiring to give the coop some light when the sun was out. David counted the chickens. There were thirteen Australorps and Bantams. He zoomed in on the footage. He saw the rooster. It was a magnificent beast with blue feathers, a puffed-out chest and the comb on the top of its head stood red and proud. It towered over the hens as it strutted around in the middle of the coop. The rooster scratched the ground with its claws, then lifted its head to the skies and crowed. The sound of the rooster crowing went through every part of David's body. He snarled in rage at the rooster in the footage.

'I'm gonna get you, you fucker,' David hissed.

David hired an excavator to come and do some work in his backyard, and the following morning a man arrived in a truck with a mini digger on the back of its tray and met David at the letterbox. They walked to the backyard and David pointed to the hedge at the fence line, then pointed to a spot on the ground and asked the excavator to go down as far as he could.

'Get as close as you can to the hedge, but don't damage it,' David instructed the excavator.

For ninety dollars an hour, the excavator didn't have a problem digging a hole close to the hedge. For the next three hours, David and Angela watched from the back door as the dirt was dug up and dumped in a pile in the middle of the yard.

'See, honey, it's easy just to sneak in at night, open the door and grab it. Anyone can do that,' David had explained to his wife. 'But they'll just get another rooster, and they might make things harder. Like they might buy a padlock and lock the gate or set up cameras. I thought I could put some Ratsak pellets into corn kernels and throw them over the fence, but I don't want to kill the chickens. I think a tunnel underneath is a safer option. I'll make a base that will blend into the ground. It will be very hard to spot, and it will be always there for us. And it will fuck with these idiots' minds. They'll be wondering to themselves, how did our rooster disappear?'

The hard work began when the excavator left. There was a big hole in the yard that went down two metres and was about three metres across. David just had to tunnel three metres underneath the hedge and then come up inside the coop. He was going to make a base from wood and glue the shavings to it and make it into a lid. He'd thought he'd spend his holidays painting, buying plants or playing with grout and cement. Instead, he was going to dig a tunnel into his neighbour's place. When he was walking the neighbourhood in the dark those three times before they moved in, he hadn't factored in this scenario.

He bought a mattock and a shovel from Bunnings. Angela made him a thermos of soup and gave it to him at the back door before he went outside. He laughed at her.

'It's not *The Great Escape*, darling.'

'This is much more important than escaping the Nazis, David.'

'Not coming out to help, baby? This affects you as much as me.'

'Didn't I tell you? I'm going out and getting my nails done.'

'Really? Since when have you ever had your nails done?'

'Since there's a tunnel that has to be dug, that's when.'

David walked outside with his mattock, shovel and thermos. He had a ladder ready, and he climbed down into the hole. It was wide enough for three people, and he didn't have to dig down any further. It was a simple equation. He just had to look to the hedge and start digging in that direction. He grabbed the mattock, raised his arm and swung it into the dirt.

He wanted to dig a burrow that was wide enough for him to crawl through. In some ways it wasn't that hard. The dirt was dark and soft, and easy to dig into. He was deep enough down that he didn't come across any roots of the hedge. He chipped away with the mattock and shovel and pushed the dirt behind him as he went. As he was digging, he heard the rooster randomly crowing on the other side of the hedge. 'I'm coming for you,' David thought, and he swung the mattock with extra vigour each time he heard the rooster crow.

After an hour, his muscles started to ache. His shirt was already covered in dirt and sweat. When Angela arrived home, he noticed her fingernails were lovely and red as she passed down containers for him to fill up with dirt. His fingernails, by contrast, were caked with black dirt. By then he had been digging for three hours. He knew he was tiring because the burrow was getting smaller and smaller. Nevertheless, before he clocked off for the day he showed off to Angela how far he had dug. His head and shoulders disappeared into the burrow.

'Wonderful, darling,' Angela said as she sat at the edge of the hole. The second day of digging he dug far enough to go in all the way to his waist, and the third day he could get his whole body in. Only his feet were showing.

After each day's digging, and after he'd showered and had his dinner, David slumped into bed wondering if it was worth the effort. Then the rooster would wake him and Angela up the next morning when it was still dark, and he knew it was.

On the fourth day, he figured he had gone far enough. He was sure he was past the hedge, and he reckoned he was under the coop, so he changed his course and started to dig up. It was too cramped and enclosed to swing a mattock, so he used a mini shovel. He had a head lamp strapped across his forehead so he could see, and he had his phone in his pocket in case dirt collapsed around him and he had to ring Angela. She came out anyway every twenty minutes or so to check on him. She would look down the hole and see flecks of dirt being kicked out of the tunnel by his feet.

On the fifth day they both slept in. They woke up at eight o'clock. They looked across to each other as they lay on their pillows, puzzled.

'What happened? Why didn't the rooster wake us up?' Angela asked David between yawns.

'I don't know. Maybe someone got to it before we did,' David joked, blinking his eyes. It was light outside. They hadn't woken up this late since they moved in.

Then, as if on cue, they heard the crowing of the rooster.

'Maybe the rooster slept in, too.'

They lay in bed, listening to the quiet of their house being punctuated by the high-pitched strangled noise of the crowing of the rooster next door. While David had been outside digging during the days, Angela had been unpacking and decorating their new house. It looked a treat. Their artwork was up, they had bought stainless-steel appliances for the kitchen, they had rugs on the floors and a new couch for the lounge room. The only thing was, their bedroom was at the back of the house instead of where they originally planned to sleep because the rooster was the loudest there.

David didn't have that much further to dig. He

was nearly done. He went down into the hole after breakfast and broke ground in the coop two hours later. He could hear the chickens.

Bok bok bok.

David stopped and used his elbows to reverse out of the hole. He went to his garage and made a base from plywood. It was two round pieces held together with hinges. He painted it black to match the colour of the dirt, then, when it had dried, he glued on the same type of wood shavings that they used next door, so the hatch would blend in with the other wood shavings on the ground.

With the hatch under his arm, he went back into the tunnel and quickly broke through the ground of the coop. He poked his head out of the hole. He had picked a good spot to dig through. He was in the corner of the coop close to the hedge. His rough calculations were spot on: he saw the feet of chickens in front of him, scratching away, oblivious to his prying eyes.

Bok bok bok.

The coop was to his left, and the rooster, the animal that had haunted them in the first week of their new home, was at the entrance of the coop. It strutted around then it cocked its head to the sky.

Cock-a-doodle-do.

David dug away with his fingers a little bit more, then he brought the hatch up, unfolded the two sides then pushed it through the open hole and laid it on the ground. It covered the hole perfectly. Just as he was wedging the hatch into the dirt, he saw the rooster glaring at him. With a flourish, the rooster spread its wings, widened its legs and charged at David. He quickly brought the hatch down on the ground. He could hear the rooster pecking on the hatch above him. Despite the incessant pecking, the hatch held its place. David shimmied back down, his smile as wide as the tunnel. He had done it. Later on in the night, when everyone was asleep, David was going to crawl through the tunnel, flip the hatch, sneak up on the unsuspecting rooster as it slept, then he was going to wrap his hands around the rooster's neck and squeeze the life out of it.

David rubbed his hands with glee as he went back inside to tell Angela the good news. He went to the bedroom at the back and saw Angela had rearranged things again. The bed was gone, the room was empty.

He went to the front of the house, opened the door of the bedroom they had first used, and found Angela sitting at the edge of the bed. The room was lit with scented candles, red rose petals scattered on the floor. Angela had done a great job of putting the bedroom together. The bed was assembled, the matching side tables were up and the expensive closet they had bought but never put together was in the corner of the room. There were Egyptian rugs on each side of the bed. Before they had moved, they had drawn pictures of how they wanted every room. Everything in the bedroom was where it was meant to be. David looked at his wife. She was barefoot, wearing tight black jeans and the blue top he'd bought her last Christmas. The musk perfume she had on drove him crazy. She was by far the best thing he'd ever set eyes on. She handed him a glass of wine.

'Honey, I've been thinking. Maybe it's for the best if we just live with the rooster. We slept through it this morning. We'll get used to it.'

David Mackay slumped on the bed next to Angela. He'd spent days digging a tunnel, spitting out dirt and worms and flicking away spiders and centipedes that crawled across his face. He cut a dejected figure as he took a slow sip of his wine.

'Now you tell me.'

'Sorry, baby. I really am.'

'You sure, honey? I mean, I'm so close I could have it in the pot in ten minutes.'

Angela wrapped her arms around her husband and kissed him on his neck.

'I know you've put in a big effort, honey; I know how sore you are. Let me spoil you a bit. I bought some oils this afternoon. Get out of those filthy clothes. I owe you a massage. It's the least I can do.'

'I guess I can live next to a rooster, as long as I wake up next to you every morning.'

Covered in dirt, and with every muscle aching in his body, David Mackay slowly rose from the bed and began to take his clothes off.

Captain Doof Doof

I walked into the computer shop in Mosley Street in Newcastle, strode past the front counter and the aisles and down the back to the technology department. The IT guy was young, in his twenties, with light brown hair combed and parted. He was wearing a shirt displaying the store's logo on his breast pocket and was whistling to himself as he was cleaning a mobile phone.

'Tim?' I said to him. 'I'm Brian. I have a twelve-thirty appointment with you.'

Tim the IT guy put down the phone, then slowly hit the keys on his computer to check his diary.

'You do,' he said as he looked up from his screen to face me. His eyes reminded me of an ex-girlfriend's. Blue and pure, and it was hard to look away from him. 'How can I help you?'

I pulled out my iPhone and laid it on the counter.

'I'm hopeless with electronics. Can you Twitter me up?'

Tim grabbed my phone, stuck his tongue out, and started scrolling down on my phone.

'For sixty bucks an hour, I can do anything.'

As I watched Tim play with my phone, his deftness in using his fingers and thumbs to type in the numbers and letters filled me with awe. How do the younger generation do it? Their electronics never leave their sides, as though attached by an umbilical cord. I gave Tim my email, my password and phone number as he set up my Twitter account.

'What do you want to call yourself?'

'Call me "Captain Doof Doof".'

I had gone away the previous weekend, to Sydney to enjoy some peace and quiet, to relax, recharge. I spent five days in a one-bedroom apartment, sitting in front of the huge windows of the lounge room, enjoying the wonderful views of the city. I explored restaurants and cinemas, the side streets and alleys, and became more familiar with a city that I wasn't entirely unfamiliar with.

The only unpleasantness that occurred was on Friday night, my last night before going home. Some new guests next door in suite 7005 started playing loud music. It was so loud I thought it was coming from somewhere below in George Street.

I walked out of my room and put my ears to the door of the room next to me.

Above the voices I heard, coming from the room,

Doof, doof.

Doof, doof.

It was way louder in my room than in the corridor. I decided on an early dinner so caught the lift and went down to the lobby. Before I went outside, I stopped at reception and lodged a complaint about my neighbours. The receptionist was very attentive, writing down the room number on her note pad, and she informed me that she'd get the hotel's security onto it. I wasn't expecting much. I'd already prepared myself for a night of interrupted sleep. I thanked her, then headed out the glass doors.

Ten minutes later I was back in the lobby, waiting for a lift with my dinner in a plastic bag in my hand. I looked at the screen above the elevator to see what floors the lifts were on. One of them was on my floor and was now on its descent. When the doors opened, first out was a grim-faced middle-aged man in a security uniform, with an identification lanyard around his neck, and following him were three young adults, two men and a woman. They marched behind him silently. They looked dressed for a celebration, but as their luggage trailed behind them, they didn't look like they were celebrating. It looked like they'd been evicted from their room. I thought they would have just been told to turn the music down. Maybe they'd done something more serious, like not being on the guest list, or they had drugs on them. Either way, they shouldn't have been playing their music loudly, and I hid my smile from them as they glumly walked past. I slept soundly that night and woke with the rising sun instead of being kept up all night because of the guests partying next door.

If only life was like that all the time. If only winning was so easy. If only life provided a 24-hour security guard. If only that empowerment I felt could follow me around. But the incident inspired me. I caught the train and the bus home, and the next day raided my fabric tub, dragged the sewing machine out from the closet and made my uniform, then booked an appointment with my local computer shop.

'Call me "Captain Doof Doof",' I told Tim the IT guy. 'Combating doof doof since the turn of the century. Put that in the description.'

'Your handle.'

'Whatever.'

'I can add a photo if you like.'

'Okay. Hang on a second.'

I took a step back and started to undress. I unbuckled my trousers, pulled down my pants, took off my tee-shirt and reached for the bag I'd brought in. A customer browsing in one of the aisles that sold printers glanced at me and smiled to herself.

'What are you doing?' Tim asked in puzzlement.

'I have a uniform,' I replied. 'I want to put it on.'

The uniform I'd made was a one-piece outfit, two sizes too small, salmon pink in colour, with the letters C D D embroidered in black across my chest. I changed quickly, then stood up straight against a wall behind me. Then I put my Zorro mask on, and pressed my elbows against my hips.

'Do you have a fan?' I asked.

'No,' Tim replied. 'Why?'

'So my hair can blow in the breeze. Proper superhero pose.'

'Sorry, don't have one.'

Tim took some pictures of me in my uniform, downloaded the photos he was happy with, and used one for my Twitter profile. He then showed me the Twitter page he'd set up for me. He told me that Twitter is limited to 120 characters per post. He showed me how to comment, how to reply, how to block people, how to start a thread.

I paid him his fee, waited for the receipt, then walked out of the shop still in my uniform. I drew bemused stares from the shoppers and pedestrians. I'd asked Tim not to take photos of my feet. I was still in my sandals that I wore around the house and didn't want my bare feet in the picture. I hopped in my car and headed home.

I'd been having a problem with some neighbours of mine who lived fifty metres away from me in my hometown. New people had moved into a rental in a nearby street, and their loud music travelled across an open reserve, from their rooms to mine.

Doof, doof.

Doof, doof.

They'd ignored my requests to turn the music down when I had knocked on their door on previous occasions. I found out which agent in town managed the house and took my complaint higher. They denied over the phone to the agent that it was them making the noise, and in retaliation they played the music louder.

I'd set up my Twitter account to check the tide of public opinion. Was I out of step with my thinking? Was I showing my age, my bitterness, my despondency, my weariness with life? Without submitting one tweet, I began to get followers as they told their stories and commented:

Love your name, love your uniform. Doof Doof music sucks. It should be banned.

Hate it. just hate it.

It's even louder when it's cold. How does that happen?

The police never come, and when they do, it starts up again as soon as they leave.

It was ten to one in my favour. Some replied the other way.

Get with the century, Captain. It's here to stay. Suck it up.

But the negative comments were few and far between.

I read tweets and threads of how respondents had called the police on their neighbours, how some had ripped out fuses and destroyed meter boxes. Some apartment dwellers had stopped paying their strata fees until it was sorted. People had sold up and moved because of it – there'd been violent altercations, people injured, and arrests and charges laid.

I'd made a commitment to myself that one way or another, the next time the music started in the house across the reserve, I was going over and not leaving until the music was stopped. The bundling out of the party-goers by hotel security had instilled confidence in me. The system could work.

I informed my Twitter followers of my plans. The replies and comments came soon enough.

Do it, Captain.

We're right behind you, all the way in Twitterverse, lol.

Ring the police first.

There aren't any, I'd replied. The towns too small, lol.

My followers had slowly been building. One of them told me that I was trending, even though I didn't know what that meant. I rang up Tim the IT guy to find out.

'You don't know what it means?' he asked, exasperated at my ignorance. 'It means you're popular, you dummy.'

I ironed my uniform and hung it up near the front door.

In preparation.

The music started the following Saturday. It was dark, just after eight. I was sitting on the couch, watching a League match on Kayo when I heard it.

Doof, doof.

Doof, doof.

Once you hear it you can't unhear it. It was wintertime, the windows were closed, the curtains drawn, yet it penetrated every room of my house. I waited ten minutes in case someone was getting ready to go out and the music would stop. After fifteen minutes I got my Captain Doof Doof costume off the hook by the door, squeezed into it, put on my sandals, and the last act before heading out was tying the mask around my eyes. I opened the front door and walked down the steps.

I knocked on the door of the house. It was a brick house, newish, beige, vertical blinds. There was a Toyota ute parked in the driveway, and spare tyres lay by the roller door of the garage. The music from the house was blasting, and I could hear voices and laughter above the racket. I knocked again, this time louder than before. The music stopped, I heard footsteps and the door swung open. A man in his twenties had one hand on the door handle, and in the other hand he was holding a can of Wild Turkey. He was wearing shorts, was barefoot and had a black Silverchair tee-shirt on. Pacific Island themed tattoos covered his forearms. I'd spoken to him before in my failed attempts to get him to turn the music down. He looked me up and down, studying my costume, his mouth agape. Then he took a slug of his drink, and said to me,

'What do the letters stand for?'

'Captain Doof Doof.'

'Nice. But do you think dressing up in some dumb outfit is going to make me turn the music down?'

'I'm hoping.'

The man finished his drink, then crunched his empty can in the palm of his hand and dropped it at my feet.

'Sometimes, hope is all you have.' He slammed the door in my face, and a few seconds later, the blasting music resumed.

I headed home, walked through the front gate, down the side of the house to the garage at the back, and grabbed an old cricket bat I'd had since I was a child. The blue grip of the bat was weathered and torn, and there were faded cherry marks in the middle of the bat from my teenage playing days. But the willow, crafted long ago in the seventies, was still solid enough. I walked across the reserve and back to the house and used the bat to pound on the door.

The same man answered. The door swung open with more force than before, as if he was expecting me. He was clutching another can of Wild Turkey. With both hands, I swung the bat at him. He anticipated my move, grabbed the bat mid-air with his free hand, yanked it from me, threw it on the ground then grabbed my chest and pulled me inside.

'Hey Bulldog,' the man yelled after he'd thrown me against the couch of the lounge room. 'This is the guy who's been dobbing us in. Come have a look at this dickhead. He looks like a walking dildo.'

Another man emerged from the kitchen. Taller and stronger than the first man, he was thin and mean-looking, his face was gaunt, his teeth crooked. It wouldn't surprise me if he was shooting up the meth he was cooking in his kitchen. I didn't get a chance to poke my head in and see if he was doing both. At first he seemed bemused at my outfit, then his mood changed to anger as he charged at me: it didn't look like he was going to read me a bedtime story.

Most people have a plan, at least until they get a punch in the head. I didn't even have a plan. I just had a stupid costume and a cricket bat lying on the floor. None of them did me any good. The first man didn't even put down his can of bourbon, he just hit me with quick jabs in between gulps of his drink, and he left it to the second man to do most of the damage. I was spun around where I stood in the lounge and was easy pickings. Blood spilt from my nose and mouth, and by the time I was pushed out the door, with laughter ringing in my ears, my face was bloodied, my jaw and cheek bones were bruised, and my head was reeling. The final humiliation was when they hurled my cricket bat at me while I was stumbling around outside. It collected me in the back of my neck and sent me sprawling onto the ground.

'Ha, ha, ha.'

I stood up, brushed the grass and dirt off my costume, grabbed the bat and dragged it glumly behind me as I walked onto the nature strip. I didn't feel like going home, so I decided to go to the bowling club across the road. I trod up the front steps, the automatic doors slid open, and I headed to the bar. It was a quiet Saturday night. A few patrons were playing billiards, a few were watching the races. Not far off closing time, the night's diners had long since left, and the restaurant staff were cleaning the tables. The sole bartender was wiping glasses with a tea towel and in bewilderment watched me approach him. I sat at a stool in front of him.

'One of those nights, hey?' he said to me. 'What'll you have?'

I ordered a gin, wiped blood from my face, then pulled out my phone and tweeted to my followers that Captain Doof Doof was a bust, and that I'd have to come up with something better.

Words of encouragement followed.

Don't give up.

It's worth pursuing.

You tried. That's something.

I could hear the music from the house booming throughout the bowling club as the bartender placed my drink on the mat in front of me. Neither the bartender, nor the pool players, nor the punters watching the races on the television seemed bothered by it. As I drank from my glass I wondered, would I become immune to the noise like them? Dulled and dimmed by time and age? Despite the pain and stress I suffered because of the loud music, I didn't want to.

The renovation

Ted Lavender was at the computer desk, rifling through the drawers, looking for the password book. He had lost it and was a bit frustrated. He remembered he had it a couple of days back when he was paying some bills online. He went to grab it again to pay for some toll notices from his last trip to Sydney, but the password book wasn't there. He began rummaging in the big drawer of the computer desk, the shelves near the floor, and the shelves on the top of the desk to his left. The drawers and shelves were full of stamps, staplers, loose bits of paper, old laptops, blank computer discs, pens, pencils, a measuring tape, screwdriver kits, Stanley knives, paper clips, sticky tape, as well as a lot of other stuff that was probably better off in the bin, but he couldn't find the password book. The book was full of passwords for banking and phone services, superannuation accounts, streaming networks, his Apple ID, social media passwords. The usual shit. He had his two daughters' banking details as well, everybody's ATO passwords and everybody's mobile numbers. He was perplexed. Your password book should only be at the one spot in the house: in a drawer by the computer. Ten times out of ten, that's where it should be. But he wasn't worried that all their personal details would be in someone else's possession. He had just put the book somewhere he shouldn't have. *It will turn up in a day or two,* he thought. *It can't have gone very far.* He shrugged his shoulders and pulled his phone from his pocket. He had to register as a visitor for the toll company or they'd charge him extra on his recent Sydney trip. He had to wait for a confirmation text, and then reset his password. It didn't take long. Still, he would have preferred to have his password book in front of him, to save him the inconvenience of having to muck around and reset his password.

When he walked in the door two days later and he saw his youngest daughter Della searching for the password book because she needed to log into something on her iPad, he knew it might become an issue.

After his cup of tea, he helped Della go through all the drawers and the shelves of the computer desk again. They pulled out the desk to see if it had slipped behind and fallen to the back against the wall. They widened their search, to see if it was amongst the photos in the living room, the bookcases in the lounge room, or if Ted Lavender had accidentally plonked it somewhere else. After twenty minutes of solid searching throughout the house, they still couldn't find it.

'Sorry, love,' Ted said to Della, shaking his head. 'I don't know where I put it.'

'That's alright, Dad. It will turn up.'

Ted came home the next day from work and was about to slot the key in his door, when he saw his neighbour, Trent, making his way towards him. They'd had a falling out a few years back and didn't communicate that much. Ted tried to avoid all the neighbours, not just Trent, as much as he could. It's not that he didn't like them, he just liked keeping himself to himself. But it was a bit hard to avoid one of his neighbours when their front door was only a metre from their fence. So once in a while, he said hello to Trent if he was in his yard.

The falling out was because Trent's dogs barked a lot. Way too much for Ted's liking. Back then Trent kept on fobbing off Ted's concerns about the nuisance that the dogs were making, by telling Ted that they were 'hyper vigilant'. That was a lousy excuse as to why the neighbour's dogs were barking all hours of the day. Ted thought 'fucking yappers' was a more apt description. He got sick of hearing the barking of his neighbour's dogs, so one day when he came home, sweating and sticky after a day's toil in the sun, and the first thing he heard when he shut the car door was the dogs yapping, he went to Trent's house, unclipped the side gate and corralled the two small dogs through the doggy door at the back door, then snibbed the door shut so they couldn't get back out. He knew Trent and his wife, Evie, were working so he pulled a pen and a scrap piece of paper from his pocket, wrote what he had done, then wrote further that if it kept on happening, he would do it again. Then he went home, had his cup of tea and waited. Trent came over when he got home from work, thumping on the door, pointing his finger, note in hand. 'How dare you?' he yelled to Ted, his voice full of anger and tension. He had called the police, he informed Ted; he also informed Ted that he was a prick then he stormed off. Sure enough, the police came a few hours later and gave Ted a warning that if it happened again, he'd be arrested for trespassing. 'Fair enough,' he told the cops. After that incident, the neighbours' dogs didn't bark as much. Evie refused to talk to Ted, but he wasn't worried. He had a win. Sometimes you have to be a bit crazy to get things to go your own way. Not big crazy, just little crazy. Rattle people a bit. Ted's wife and daughters had been out shopping when it happened, so they had no idea what he'd done nor of the subsequent visit from the police. Ted felt no inclination to tell them. He felt his act of spontaneity had paid off.

Ted was seeing a lot more of Trent now, though. The neighbours were getting renovations done to their house. They were enclosing their verandah at the front and getting a garage built close to the fence, so he'd seen Trent a fair bit over the last couple of months, as he was outside talking to the builders, cleaning up or shovelling dirt out of the way.

And now, here Trent was, with his cap on backwards, bounding from the front of the garage towards Ted. It was like Trent was waiting for him to come home. Ted quickly jiggled the keys in the door. He'd had a rough day and the last thing he wanted was a chit-chat with the neighbour he didn't like. But he wasn't quick enough. Trent rested his elbows on the fence and confronted him.

'Why did you do it, Ted?'

This was new. He turned and saw Trent had an aggressive look on his face. He looked like he wanted to spit on Ted.

'Sorry?' Ted asked. 'What do you mean?'

'Why did you do it?' Trent repeated.

Ted forgot about opening the door and walked down to his side of the fence and faced Trent.

'What are you talking about, Trent?'

There was fury all over Trent's face: his eyebrows were drawn in a frown, and he looked pained.

'Someone dobbed us into council for not getting a DA.'

'What makes you think it was me?' Ted asked.

'Because of our history with the dogs, I just assumed it was you.'

'Well, it wasn't.'

They spent the next few minutes having a strained conversation. Acting on a complaint, a council worker had been over at Trent's place last Friday, talking to his builders. Work had to grind to a halt while the approval process began. If it was approved, they'd have to replace their new windows and construct a concrete driveway in front of the garage. It was going to cost them a few thousand dollars to come up to code. There was also a 42-day delay because of the complaint. Ted professed his innocence three or four times, then the conversation drew to an end when Trent walked away from Ted and went inside his house, as if he'd had enough of hearing Ted's excuses, leaving Ted just standing there on his own.

A few minutes later he heard Trent mucking around with a drill in his garage and he had his music up loud, which was a first. Ted reckoned Trent carried the traits of an inner-city hipster. A smug, vainglorious, know-it-all. He used to see Evie practising her yoga in the back yard, standing on one leg like a crane standing in water. Ted thought they were the ultimate hipster couple.

Ted then heard Evie, who had joined her husband in the garage, sing along loudly in a high-pitched voice to the music. That was a first, too. Ted felt sorry for them. They were angry at what had happened to them, but didn't know where to direct their anger. *Just don't direct it my way,* Ted thought as he turned away from his bedroom blind. He did ponder though, why didn't they just submit a development application? They were getting a lot of work done. A new garage, an enclosed verandah; there were builders there all the time. If someone was strolling past or walking their dog and didn't like what they were seeing and wanted to cause some mischief, Trent and Evie were sitting ducks. But the work looked legitimate to Ted. He thought it was obvious that Trent and Evie would have applied for a DA.

He told his wife, Maree, what had happened when she arrived home from work.

'Was it you?' she asked him as she placed the groceries on the kitchen bench.

'Of course not,' he replied, hurt at the suggestion.

His eldest daughter Emma came home from work. He told her what happened as well.

'They think it was me,' Ted finished.

'That makes sense,' Emma shot back as she closed the pantry door and headed to her bedroom.

Bloody hell, not even my own family believes me, Ted thought.

His youngest daughter, Della, came home from school five minutes later. When he saw Della, it reminded him that she'd been looking for the password book the day before. While Maree started preparing dinner, he spent the next fifteen minutes again searching in vain for the password book.

That night in bed, while Maree played games on her phone, Ted stewed. He felt wronged that he was blamed. That meant the builders, when they returned, and the neighbours would think it was him as well. Trent and Evie would get all the sympathy, while Ted would get the silent and accusing stares from everyone. Maree saw him stewing, turned off her phone and faced him.

'What's wrong, honey?' she asked him.

'I don't like being blamed for something I didn't do,' he complained. 'You don't even believe me.'

'Well, honey, you do have a history of doing things like that. You did nearly get arrested for jumping the fence and locking their dogs inside.'

'How did you know about that?'

'I was speaking with Evie a couple of days after it happened. The girls know about it, too. Remember the Andersons across the road with their wood heater? You got the environmental arm of council onto them.'

'Their wood heater stunk,' Ted protested. 'It was a kerosene heater. For ten months of the year our house stunk of kerosene. It was terrible.'

'It was pretty bad,' Maree conceded.

'Had to do something, love. And Trent and Evie's dogs were terrible back then. They drove me crazy.'

'I know. It's funny. Being blamed for something you didn't do. It doesn't bother you getting blamed for something you did do. Funny. Don't let it worry you. I feel sorry for them.'

'Okay. Alright. Well, goodnight.'

They kissed each other goodnight, and five minutes later Maree was asleep. Ted had nearly nodded off when he heard Trent and Evie's dogs yapping. They stopped and Ted fell asleep, only to be wakened by them barking again five minutes later. Ted decided, as he rolled around on his side of the bed, that while he had felt sorry for them fifteen minutes ago, he didn't now. The dogs stopped barking after a few minutes. Ted knew that they were just having a last run in the backyard before going in for the night. *If I was a cynical man,* Ted thought, *Trent got the dogs to do a bit of extra barking just to piss me off.*

The next day Ted was at the desk as he searched forlornly one more time for the password book. He had basically given up by now and had grabbed another exercise book and had started rewriting the passwords he remembered into the new book as he went.

An idea formed in his head. He went on his computer, went on Google and spent a few minutes surfing the web. Then he made his phone call.

'Alwyn Investigations. Pete Morelli speaking.'

Ted Lavender explained the situation that had happened next door a few days back, how he was blamed for something he didn't do, and was wondering if someone could make some investigations on his behalf. Ted wanted to know who had complained to council so he could clear his name and then use it to shove it up Trent's fucking arse.

'Who's your local council?' Pete from Alwyn Investigations asked.

Ted told him.

'Okay. We might be able to help you there. We've done this kind of work with this council before. It might take a few days, but it shouldn't be a problem. There's a five-hundred-dollar retainer, payable up front, and I reckon it will be about fifteen hundred all up.'

Ted mulled the sum in his head. It was steeper than he thought it would be, but he could afford it. Pete obviously knew someone on the inside, and the $1500 would be split between Alwyn Investigations and the council insider. It was just a matter of the insider logging on and checking all the records involved in the matter. A simple ten-minute process at most, and $1500 seemed to be the going rate.

'Okay, I'm in.'

Ted gave his credit card details; he heard Pete's fingers punching in the numbers.

'All good,' Pete said. 'Now, what's the address of your neighbours? I'll get onto it as soon as I hang up the phone. It might be done this afternoon, but more likely it will take a day or two.'

Ted heard Pete write down the address, then they said goodbye and Ted hung up. Ted was glad. He had done the right thing. He rose from the computer chair to go outside and check the mail. As he got to the front door, he looked through the glass panels and saw Trent pottering about outside his garage, shovelling around some uneven dirt. Evie was in the background, tipping some rubbish into the bin. Ted groaned. He shelved the idea of walking outside to his letterbox and retreated back inside his house. He didn't want to see Trent. He thought in the future he might need to get some privacy screens going along the top of the fence. He didn't particularly want to see someone who had accused him of doing something he didn't do. As he walked back from the front door to his lounge room, he realised he couldn't wait to hear back from Pete of Alwyn Investigations.

***

Ted had nearly finished his new passwords for his new book. What passwords he couldn't remember, he went through the rigmarole of creating new passwords, a few minutes each day after work. He called out to his girls and Maree, and they stood behind him at the computer desk as they helped him with their details.

He wrote down the password for a newspaper he subscribed to, and he was done. He had finished his new password book. He closed the cover and emphasised to his wife and daughters that the book was never to be moved from the computer drawer under the keyboard.

'Rightio, dad,' Della said to him with a smile on her face. 'It's our fault we lost it.'

He ignored her remark, placed the new password book in the drawer and slid it closed. *Fuck the lot of ya's,* he thought. But he was smiling too. It was done.

He'd actually had a good couple of days filling out his new password book. He'd hung out with his daughters a bit as he pestered them to hand over their passwords and codes. They'd protested that all their information was on their phones, but he'd convinced them it was always good to have a bit of backup. They'd reluctantly agreed. He didn't see that much of them anymore, so it was always good to catch up with them, even if it was something as mundane as chasing them up for some codes and passwords for their electronics.

He tapped the drawer for good luck.

Ted thought, *I hope I never have to do that again.*

The next day, Ted Lavender was going through the small drawer by his bedside, going through his old documents and bills, seeing what was okay to throw out or keep for another couple of months. It was his system. He held onto bills for about a year and then threw them away. An old rates notice from six months back slipped off the bed. It floated like a feather and landed behind the drawer. He reached down blindly to retrieve the notice when his hand struck something solid that was standing against the wall.

What the fuck?

He had an ominous thought and in one swift move he pulled up his old password book.

What the hell?

He turned the password book over in his hands. There was a thin layer of dust covering it.

How did this end up here?

Why would I put it there?

Were the girls messing with me?

Ted Lavender sat on the edge of his bed in a flustered state. He scratched his head, his brain ticking over. He couldn't remember putting the book behind the drawer at all. He knew his girls wouldn't muck him around like this; he was in no doubt it was him as he was the only one who used the book to pay the bills. But why would he do that? Ted was confused.

The phone rang. He put his troubles aside for the moment and reached into his pocket.

'What type of caper you pulling here, Lavender?' It was Pete Morelli from Alwyn Investigations. He sounded agitated and angry.

'Sorry, Pete. What are you talking about? Have you found it who it was that called council on the neighbours?'

'Yeah, we found out.' Pete's tone relaxed a bit. There was a shred of sympathy in his voice. 'First off, give us your credit card details again. I'm only charging a thousand instead of fifteen hundred, so the balance is five hundred.'

Ted reached into his wallet and read the numbers down the line. He heard the Eftpos machine printing out the receipt.

'Well, who was it?' Ted Lavender asked Pete Morelli.

'Who was it? You want to know who it was? It was you, that's who it was.'

'What?'

'Ted, it was you who rang up and lodged the complaint with council. I have the time you lodged the complaint. It was a Thursday afternoon, just after three. You gave your name, your address, your mobile. It's all in the report in front of me. You said something dodgy was going on with the next door's renovations, and maybe it would be a good idea if council investigated.'

There was a pause.

'Are you okay, Ted?'

Ted Lavender pulled the phone away from

his ear and hung up on Pete Morelli from Alwyn Investigations.

Ted was in shock. No way was it him. Surely, he'd remember doing something as serious as calling council over the neighbours' renovations. *What caper was I trying to pull? Pete Morelli asked me. More like what caper was Alwyn Investigations trying to pull? That was a waste,* Ted thought. *What a gyp.* He'd just blown $1000 on a bogus investigation.

He looked down at the old bills and documents still on his bed. He'd forgotten why they were there. Then he saw his password book resting by the pillows.

What's this doing here? Ted thought. It belonged in the drawer in the computer desk. He stood up, grabbed the password book and headed out of his bedroom.

Futsal

The referee blew his whistle from the sidelines and the match commenced. The opposition player with the ball on the line at his feet quickly passed it to his teammate. They did the old one-two, sidestepped my teammates like they were slicing butter and steamed towards me like runaway locomotives. I put my hands out and spread my feet to no avail. From a few metres out the locomotive on the left fired the ball like a bullet and it rocketed past me into the back of the net. I checked the timeclock above the net when I went to retrieve the ball. The game had been going for fourteen seconds. I rolled the ball back to my team in the middle of the court. My teammate Chris was in the centre of the court, already hunched over from chasing the two players for ten seconds. His grey locks spilt down his sides, and he looked he was about to have three aneurisms at once. He took deep breaths as he rested his hands on the top of his pulled-up footy socks.

We kicked off, lost possession to one of their defenders, who dribbled the ball down the side, then flicked it into the middle of the court. There was an opening; the other locomotive pounced like a gazelle, ran a few steps, the rocket was fired, and into the corner of the net the ball went. A minute had passed.

2–0.

'Guys,' I pleaded to my already exhausted teammates. 'A bit of backup.'

Futsal wasn't really our game – we were cricket mates. Some of us missed hanging out with each other like we did during the summer months, so I put my hand up to come up with something for us to do during winter. I had a choice between darts played every Tuesday at the Family Hotel, trivia at the bowling club every Monday, or table tennis on Monday evenings at the scout hall. Croquet was played in a local park but that was played in the mornings during work hours. I even thought of us playing the chess tournaments that were held on Saturday mornings at the library. But, after I went for a swim at the aquatic centre one day after work, I saw a flyer inviting players to form their own teams for the local futsal competition and thought, why not? I rang my cricket mates and asked them, 'What do you reckon?'

A week later I registered us in fifth division and named our team 'the Adoraballs'. I put the word out to all my cricket mates, but only four turned up for the first game of the new season. You were allowed five on a court, and if we could only muster three, we would have to forfeit. The team we were playing, with the youthful rocket-shooting locomotives, were called 'Lord of the Wings'.

The ref blew his whistle to recommence play. We passed the ball straight to one of their players, he ran at me like he had four legs instead of two and the ball cannoned into the back of the net. 3–0. He even had time to give me a sly smile as he thundered towards me. *I should have chosen darts,* I thought as I picked up the ball from the back of the net.

My teammates were standing in the middle of the court, hands on hips, red-faced and panting, as I rolled the ball along the ground to them. They were probably thinking I should have chosen darts as well.

Three minutes had passed. Another thirty-three to go.

The whistle blew and we kicked off. The ball was passed to opening batsman Walter. He went to kick the ball forward, missed, flew in the air like a drunken ballerina then fell on his arse. The opposition pounced. They passed the ball to each other like a pinball as they ran down the court. Five seconds later, I was fishing the ball out of the back of the net again.

I hadn't known how fast-paced a game futsal was. We were all in our forties, ridiculously unfit and the years of indulgence, inactivity and our lack of coordination finally caught up with us on court 2 at the Katoomba aquatic centre. In previous decades we used to be slim, even half fit. Time had taken its toll, brutally in some cases. At least with cricket if you sprinted to the fence to prevent a boundary and were a bit puffed you could hide at third man or in the slips for a while as you recovered. There was nowhere to hide during a game of futsal. If you fell on the ground playing cricket, at least you fell onto soft mown grass. The floor of the futsal court was wooden parquetry and hard as concrete.

The other team took pity on us in the second half, lent us one of their players and the game petered out. Even so, we didn't have one shot on goal. We lost 18–0. It should have been 30–0. My reflexes had kicked in occasionally and I made some half-decent saves, more from self-preservation than skill. After what seemed an eternity, the buzzer went to end the game. We shook hands with the victors and were barely able to hobble our way to the chairs at the sides. Once there, we sat in stone-cold silence, too sore to move, too stunned and melancholic to speak. None of us had expected such a hectic workout.

Gradually the voices of pain and sorrow emerged.

'My knees,' wailed one of my teammates. 'My back,' moaned another. I had landed awkwardly on my elbow in a doomed attempt to save a goal and already it was purple and bruised.

'What were you fucking thinking, Norman?' Ronny, our wicket keeper, said to me outside the entrance. We were a circle of misery as we stood by the bus stop, having a smoke before we went home. 'That was fucked.'

'Yeah, Norman,' Walter snorted. 'It will take me a week to recover.'

'We have to think of a strategy,' I countered. 'Maybe come up with some forward plays. Work out who can defend?'

My teammates flung their smokes into the bush in disgust, left me and shuffled into the darkness towards the car park.

'See you next week then?' I asked them, my voice filled with hope. None of them replied.

My teammates texted me through the next few days.

Still sore, Norman.

Idiot.

I can't even lift my arm to have a drink.

How did you end up goalkeeper?

The following week I wasn't sure if any of them were going to turn up. I chatted to the secretary of the organisation after paying the match fees as I nervously waited. Then one by one, I saw my teammates drift in, the smell of Dencorub and Tiger Balm trailing after them.

We were playing a team called 'the Misfits'. Their average age looked to be about twenty-two but they were as uncoordinated as us and for a while it was a contest. Our off-spinner Carl had joined so we had a full team. The Misfits only had one good player, a thin and athletic type who could run all day, but that was all they needed, and they won 11–0. I could tell as I watched while I was guarding the net they had played together for a while, and while they relied on the one good player to win the game for them, he relied on his teammates just as much with their placement of the ball to set him up for his strikes.

'We should practise together,' I said to my teammates as we stood outside by the bus stop, having a cigarette before heading home.

'Fuck that,' said Ronny, our fast bowler who'd had a couple of wide shots on goal. 'It takes me all week to recover.'

My teammates flicked their cigarettes into the ground and went home, leaving me on my own again.

The following week we played a team called 'Man Chest Hair United', and lost 16–0. This team didn't have one good player, they had three. We never stood a chance. The other teams we played seemed to have lots of fun, but there was no joy in it for us.

When we were out the front, swallowing anti-inflammatory pills while we smoked our cigarettes, Chris, our first drop, suggested maybe it wasn't a bad idea to practise a little bit.

The following Saturday morning we met at the cricket nets at the local park, and instead of cricket balls, bats and wickets, I'd brought a couple of soccer balls. For thirty minutes we practised on the grass by the nets, passing the ball to each other. We settled on who would defend and who would be our strikers. Minor details that should have been figured out before we played.

The following Wednesday we played a team called the 'Sir Percy's'. Walter kicked off, passed it to Chris, who from fifteen metres out lifted his back leg and foot, and booted the ball. Their goalie was still napping, and the ball shot into the back of the net. There were whoops of joy from all of us.

Our first goal.

We were in front for a minute. Then one of their players wearing an Arsenal jumper levelled. Two minutes later they were in front and went further ahead as the game wore on. I made some good saves. I enjoyed being the goalkeeper. It was my one condition of organising the team, paying the registration costs for my mates, buying shin pads for everyone. If I stumped up the cash, I was staying in goal. I was the most unfit of all of us. I would be most at risk of having a heart attack from running around the court. I would be most at risk of falling headfirst onto the hard wooden floor.

I tried to anticipate where the ball was going to go when they were coming towards me. I watched the footwork of the approaching players to see when they were going to shoot for goal and what part of the net they were aiming for. By now I had gloves and knee pads to help me be more mobile. My wide girth helped me make some decent saves, but it still wasn't enough.

'That was a better effort, boys,' I said to them all when we were outside, having our after-game cigarettes.

'We lost eleven–one,' Ronny chimed in. 'How is that better?'

'I see improvement. I see us getting fitter and our game improving. Don't you?'

'Not much.'

It became apparent to all of us when we were thrashed 20–0 by ladder leader of division 5, 'Notts Florist', the next game, that no amount of training at the park by the nets on the weekend would help us. We were old, we had no soccer skills, on court we were like elephants tip-toeing through a field of land mines. Futsal wasn't for us. We decided, as we were smoking our cigarettes by the bus shelter after the match, that we'd play one more game then forfeit the rest of the season. I couldn't argue with them. I felt guilty about putting them in a situation they couldn't handle. But they'd turned up for four matches. At least they'd had a go.

I was walking down Katoomba Street the following afternoon when I spotted a driver's licence lying in the gutter near a drain outside the local café. I picked it up, twirled it in my hands, and wondered how it ended up in a Katoomba gutter. There was no wallet nor any other cards. The licence belonged to a P-plater from Penrith. Male, fresh-looking, born in this century with a confident smile that only the young can get away with. I kept on walking down Katoomba Street, past the laundromat, then the youth hostel, and walked into the police station. I handed the licence to the police officer manning the front desk and walked back out.

I had just passed the youth hostel on my way back to town when an idea formed. *Is it worth it?* I wondered. *For one last game?* I shrugged my shoulders and walked through the doors of the hostel. *What have I got to lose?*

On game day, I waited until Ronny, the last of the Adoraballs, arrived. On the noticeboard next to the shower block were the ladders of the various divisions. We were winless and last in division 5. But I had a surprise to spring.

I'd put up a notice at the hostel after visiting the police station. Katoomba has always been a tourist town. In its early days it mined coal but once that dried up, the cooler climate and the clifftop views have attracted visitors for over a hundred years. Tourists come from all parts of Australia, and from all parts of the world. In most of those countries the overseas tourists hailed from, soccer was their national sport.

After Ronny had signed on at the desk, I sprang my surprise.

'Fellas, meet our new recruits, Tomas, Patrick and Ferdinand.' I motioned the three, who were standing by the cleaner's room, to make their way over.

Ferdinand had rung me on behalf of the trio. None of them thought anyone played soccer in Australia. They had hooked up when they were in Melbourne and were backpacking together around the country. Tomas was from Dusseldorf, Patrick from York and Ferdinand from Glasgow. They were staying in the mountains for a few months, working as labourers while they saved up enough cash to head up to Queensland. They were in their twenties, lean and wiry, their limbs fresh, and they looked keen to play.

I introduced them to the team, filled out their paperwork, paid the match fees to the secretary and we headed down to court 2.

We were playing the Sir Percy's, the team against which we had led briefly before getting swamped. It was the early game, the first game for the night, so the other team had brought their kids with them and the court was flooded with children in their school uniforms playing and kicking balls around the court.

We warmed up amongst the mayhem. I was in the goals, feeding the ball to my teammates who were in an arc in front of me. For the first time, we had more than five players, which meant that we would have three reserves. Tomas, Ferdinand and Patrick trained like they were born kicking a soccer ball. They passed with precision; their kicks for goal, even casual shots, were right on target and thumped into my stomach.

The ref blew his whistle to let everyone know kick-off was imminent. The kids were shooed off the court and everyone went to their positions. Chris, Donny and Carl were the first reserves. Our European trio were up front while Walter was in front of me in defence. The whistle blew and the game began. Ferdinand passed it to Tomas, who moved forward and kicked the ball to himself as he weaved the ball between the legs of his opponents.

He saw that Patrick was on his own in the middle of the court; Tomas passed the ball, and Patrick, from five metres out, drilled the ball into the back of the net.

Like the first time we played against this team, we scored in the first minute. This time, though, they didn't level the scores in the next minute. In fact they didn't come close to scoring throughout the match. Such were the supreme skills of our new players, they bamboozled the other team with their prowess and scored at will. They ran like rabbits, tackled tirelessly, and were deadly shots on goal. Their footwork was magical to watch. They made us oldies look like we dragged anvils when we chased after the ball.

Walter and I were reduced to spectators, having no defending to do, and at half time we led 7–0. The Sir Percy's players on their bench at the other end of the court looked ragged and flustered. I could hear the chorus of bickering from them. Clearly they'd expected another easy win. Walter and I had a break for the second half as Chris and Donny took our positions. The ref set the clock, then blew his whistle. Play commenced.

We won 15–0. I wasn't required for the second half, neither was Walter, and Carl wasn't required at all. Each goal was more anticlimactic than the last. Even though we were going to win easily, I didn't think it was much of a match. My new teammates belonged in a much higher division, and everyone who was watching knew it. I suspected it was the cause of the opposition's frustrations at the half-time break.

The match ended, the players congregated in the middle and shook hands. We should have been jumping for joy at our first win. Instead it was a subdued affair as my teammates walked towards us at the bench.

After we packed up, I thanked the three recruits for their contribution, and they followed us out to the front door. They'd been running around for thirty-six minutes and hadn't even broken into a sweat. They didn't even look tired. They bade us farewell as we reached for our cigarettes by the bus stop, and we watched them as they walked the car park to Patrick's battered Hyundai.

'What the fuck were you thinking, Norman?' Carl demanded.

'Yeah, you idiot,' Chris added.

'What are you talking about?' I asked, dumbfounded. 'We had a win. What's the problem?'

'We've been thinking,' Walter explained. 'It's not as bad as we've made it out to be. We actually enjoy it, even though we're getting thrashed every week. It's not that different to cricket. We hang out together every week and lose. But winning like we just did is no fun. I'd rather get thrashed than win like that. So we decided while we were packing up, that we might continue on.'

'I played rugby league for Bega when I was a

teenager,' Chris said. 'Never won a game for four years. Had a great time.'

'Did you tell the secretary we were forfeiting the rest of the season?' Ronny asked.

I shook my head. 'I was just planning on none of us turning up.'

'Okay, we'll keep going. Just the five of us. No imports. I doubt we'll win a game, but who cares? You okay with that, Norman? This was your idea after all.'

I looked from face to face as they waited for my reply. 'So you're okay with the thrashings then?' I asked them all.

'We're okay with the thrashings,' Walter replied. The others nodded in agreement.

'Okay. Then we'll keep on playing.'

I watched them flick their cigarettes into the bush by the bus stop, pick up their bags and walk to their cars.

We'd hung out together on cricket pitches and at pubs for years. We'd enjoyed BBQs and drinks in each other's backyards and watched our kids grow up. They'd been a part of my life for fifteen years.

I was supremely glad I was their friend. I'd sprung a surprise with the three recruits before the match but their surprise afterwards, outside in the cold by the bus shelter as we smoked our cigarettes, when they told me they wanted to keep going, was the better one.

Stone

The loudspeaker crackled into life. The manager's voice blasted from inside his office, 'Tools down, people. I have a briefing.'

The rollers on the conveyor belt slowed to a halt. The ball bearings stopped rattling and we stood by our frames. 'What is it this time?' we grumbled to each other. My mate pointed to the side of my steel mesh frame. Over the weekend a safety message had been upgraded and there was a new metal hazard sign on our frames. Under the warnings and notes of caution, there was a barcode with a cage ID number, and next to the web address of the company that produced the frames, was one word: 'Compactainer'.

'What the fuck does that word even mean?' my co-worker asked me. It was written on the bottom of the sign on his frame too. I was about to give a smart-arse response, but the loudspeaker drowned out my reply.

'Listen up, people,' the manager began. His door shut, he sat in his chair in front of his computer with his mic in hand. His voice boomed from the loudspeaker placed above his office door, the sound carrying throughout the factory. We didn't even get a good morning. Our manager had a voice like the DVD commentary of a movie you didn't want to watch. 'I've just received some information that's come down the line to run through. It's to do with the wearing of masks during this latest outbreak of Covid. First off, thanks for everyone wearing masks. There haven't been too many problems up here. Everyone's complying, so thank you.

'This is a new policy announcement in regard to the masks we wear in our workforce. It's become apparent that some employees are wearing masks that carry political messages. The union has sent out masks to their members with their logo on it which some of you have been wearing. It breaches the company's policy regarding political content, so after today, they're banned from all worksites. The company has manufactured our own masks, so that's the preferred mask we'd like you to wear. Other acceptable masks are plain ones with no messaging at all. Colourful ones, rainbow ones, even masks in your favourite football team colours are acceptable, but not union masks. Thank you, people. Back to work.'

It always happened. The faint praise, then the slam.

The manager's name was Glen Stone. Covid had been good to him. It had handed him more control, more power and authority, which he loved. Another stick to flog us with. He was a control freak who had to have things go his way. He told me once, when we were having a discussion about some workplace disagreement, 'You all think I'm an arsehole, but I look after you blokes more than you think.' 'Pig's fucking arse, you are a fucking arsehole,' I muttered under my breath. He was one of those managers that once he was after someone, didn't let up, and so we all tried to fly under the radar. His sole skill seemed to be lying and scheming his way into a nice, comfortable office chair, a higher position, a higher pay grade, then doing as little as possible for as long as he could. When things weren't going his way and he became angry, spit dribbled from the side of his mouth, his face looked like a beetroot and his head looked like it was going to burst. He slammed doors and walked around the factory with a scowl on his face that would scare wild animals. Sometimes he would swivel in his chair, glaring out from the office windows, just waiting for us to commit some misdemeanour he could ping us with. There weren't many of us, so it was hard to hide sometimes. We were semi-rural, on the outskirts of the city. The nearest factory the company owned was fifty kilometres away, so we were stuck with each other. Even the managers from head office didn't like him: they thought he was a lazy shit. They'd even tried to transfer him to another factory on the other side of the city, just to get him out of their jurisdiction. But Stone had dug his heels in, engaged the services of a solicitor, and won his case. When he was given directives from above, he'd just flat out refuse the directive and counter with, 'I'm not doing that,' or 'that's not in my job description.' And when things were coming to a boil, like if a worker had laid a bullying or harassment charge against him, he'd go on sick leave for a few weeks, and a couple of days later after he was back, it was like he had never left, and he'd crank things up again. It was like he was untouchable, like he had inside information on the top bosses which prevented them taking any sort of action against him. He had been bullying us for years, but he was like a snake on a tree, and when things were getting tight, he would slither away. One minute he was storming out of his office to tell you off about some issue, then an hour later he'd be all chummy with you, as if nothing had ever happened. He knew how much he could get away with, and was an expert at taking advantage of our generally good natures. With Covid, he would go out of his way to find things to get us in trouble, like not sanitising or not checking in properly. Understandable in a way, but he used the social distancing rules to harass us all, even though with the job we did, it was impossible to social distance.

The last straw for me was the incident with the biscuits. With the onset of Covid, we had kept our jobs, but our overtime had disappeared. We were all down about six grand a year. We weren't complaining; we knew we were lucky compared to people unable to work at all. So, one of my workmates on the way back to the factory used to bring packets of biscuits from the local cracker factory that he delivered to, and in a nice gesture of solidarity, he would leave the packets of biscuits at our frames for us. The biscuits were rejects and were given away by the company. My co-worker would bring back Monte Carlos, Teddy Bears, Milk Arrowroots, and sometimes as a treat we'd get some Scotch Fingers or Butternut Snaps. He even left some for Stone on his desk. We nearly got a smile out of him. Stone wasn't used to being a beneficiary from any random act of kindness.

Then one day, there was a letter waiting on my workmate's desk when he returned to the factory. He opened the envelope to find he was charged with unauthorised use of the company vehicle. Even though Stone had received biscuits from him, he had done an about-turn and pinged him for using the company vehicle for bringing biscuits for his workmates. Typical of Stone.

There wasn't much my workmate could do. He couldn't contest the charges. Everyone knew he was bringing biscuits back to the factory for us. A logistics manager came up from another office and gave him a formal warning. It was now on my workmate's permanent record. If it happened again, he could face further discipline – a code of ethics inquiry, further discipline, pay reduction, dismissal. He was a bit pissed off and a bit jaded. One of the company's more infamous moments in their treatment of their staff was when a worker returned from a month's holidays, and after he clocked on, he was called into the office and given a warning for some misdemeanour dating almost two months back. Some welcome back to work.

This warning given to my workmate over a petty misdemeanour was enough for me. I'd had enough of this Stone, this shell of a man who nabbed us on the smallest of things. I wasn't the only one who had trouble dealing with him. We may have called him Mr Stone to his face, but behind his back we all called him 'Pebbles': he was small and pointless and we'd all like to stomp on him. It was a childish act of pettiness, but it was our way of coping.

We were in the middle of our latest enterprise bargaining negotiations with the company. The previous EBA had expired just before Covid struck. There was a twelve-month freeze on wage rises, but the year was up, and negotiations had recommenced. Our factory, like other factories in the company across the country, was heavily unionised. Even with declining union membership numbers, our union was one of the stronger ones in the country. There were other versions of Stones, sitting in their offices, picking on their workers. So, even if you didn't believe in unions when you started the job, you'd soon happily stump up your fortnightly dues after you'd tangled with management.

The union held fortnightly Zoom meetings to give updates to their members during the negotiations. The company was one of the few in the country that had profited during Covid, but we had given some conditions up. We had sacrificed our early start times, our overtime had dried up. The workers had adapted to working in the midst of a pandemic, and now the union was after some payback. It was a good sort of payback. The brass just wanted the EBA signed off and endorsed. Despite the argy-bargy that went on in the day-to-day operation of all its workplaces, the company realised the goodwill of its workers had pulled them through during Covid. It wasn't looking for a fight this time so had agreed to all the union's demands. We were getting a larger than usual pay rise, our penalty rates were retained, and our overtime was coming back.

The branch secretary was finishing up his Zoom information briefing. The voting forms would be mailed to members in the next couple of weeks, he said. He encouraged everyone to vote yes and thanked all the reps and the members for their help over the negotiating period. Then, like he did at the end of each Zoom meeting, he opened up the meeting to the rank and file, starting with those workers who, during the course of the meeting, had put their names down to request a chat with the branch secretary.

'I've got Carl from the Central Coast first on the list,' the branch secretary said. A vision of a middle-aged man, still in his uniform, appeared on my computer screen at the bottom corner. 'How ya going, Carl? Mate, you have to unmute so we can hear you,' the branch secretary said. We all saw Carl aim his finger to the bottom of the screen.

'Sorry, Bruce,' Carl said. 'Mate, first off I want to thank everyone at the union for all their hard work over the last few months. We really appreciate it, but management are up to their usual tricks. We got this really weird directive this morning. They've told us we're not allowed to wear union masks because they class it as political messaging. But we all know it's a blatant attempt to stop us wearing union masks.'

'Look, guys,' the branch secretary stated, 'I've been talking to state and national management on a daily basis over the last year to ensure the company remains viable and their employees and our members still have a job. I can tell you personally, the last thing they're going to be worried about is workers wearing a mask with the union's logo on it. They've got other things to worry about it. So, Carl, just ignore this shit. It's just middle management trying to justify their positions. Did other members from other factories get the same directive?'

The branch secretary paused to view the messages coming through from the reps.

'Okay. Judging from your replies, it's been read out to other offices as well. Guys, I'll tell you again, senior management couldn't give a shit. You blokes are the front-line workers. You're carrying the company through this pandemic. If they tell you to take it off, ignore them. If you get in trouble over it, we will back you up. No problems there.'

The meeting soon ended. I went to my bedroom and started rummaging through my wardrobe. I didn't think I'd even opened the envelope the union had sent that contained the mask. Eventually

I found the envelope in a top cupboard. I ripped it open, and the mask slipped into my hands. The mask was a standard mask, the same style and size that everyone else was wearing. It was red in colour with the union logo typed in black at the bottom left of the mask. I hadn't even thought about wearing the union mask. I just wore the standard disposable blue and white ones. But after the biscuit incident, and today's directive about masks, I knew what mask I was going to wear. I was up for a fight. I'd done my time putting up with the narcissistic and borderline psychopathic Stone.

The next day, I was the only one wearing a union mask when we commenced our shift. All those who were wearing union masks from the day before were now wearing generic masks. I saw the raised eyebrows of my workmates when we clocked on. They were going to see some action today. My rebellion lasted for ten minutes, then the speaker above Stone's office crackled. The great man was about to speak.

'Solomon Baxter, please report to the office immediately.'

We were barred from going into Stone's office because of Covid. He was too afraid we'd pass an infection onto him. He hadn't even liked the workers going into his office even before Covid, and now he had an excuse to keep us out. We had to walk to the side of his office, slide the glass panel and talk to him there.

Stone was at his computer in the corner, checking

his morning emails. He was wearing the company hi-vis vest. Even management's hi-vis had to be different to workers' hi-vis. While ours was the common and distinctive canary yellow, theirs was a dark red. I could see his long hair, combed with gel down the back and sides to keep it in place. We knew he was precious about his long locks. He had a mirror above his desk, and we would see him preening himself, brushing his hair several times a day. He was vain in other ways too. He had a kettle station and would lift weights as he sat in his chair.

He turned when he heard the glass panel sliding. Above his mask, his olive eyes glared at me

'Solomon,' he said. 'This is a documented discussion.' I saw Stone's computer screen in front of him. The emails had gone, and he had a blank page open. His fingers were resting on the keyboard, keen and eager to type my responses. 'Did you not hear yesterday's briefing regarding the correct procedure when it comes to the appearance of masks? The mask you are wearing now is prohibited.'

I'd been a company man for over twenty years. I'd come in when I'd been sick, helped them out when they'd been short on manpower, and changed my holidays to suit their roster, and I'd never gone out of my way to stir up trouble. People were dropping like flies from a killer disease, and I was being hauled over the coals because of the design of my mask. Standing next to the shredding bin at the glass panel as Stone waited for my response, his back to me as he had turned to the computer to record my answer, I did something I'd never done before.

I ignored my manager. Without answering Stone, I slid the glass panel back in its place and returned to my workstation. I reckon the company mask he was wearing wouldn't have prevented his jaw from falling to the floor.

When I returned to my frame after work to clock off there was a letter for me on my desk. I knew what it was before I even opened it up. It was a typed letter, signed off by Stone. I was to receive a warning and counselling in ten days' time.

There were two clauses I had breached.

Section one, clause one – Noncompliance of not wearing correct uniform – mask with political content.

Section four, clause two – Not adhering to work directives.

I rang the branch organiser of the union when I got home. He laughed when I read him out the letter.

'You're the twentieth member I've dealt with today who's going to receive a warning for wearing a mask. It's a revolution.'

'What should I do?'

'Don't do anything. I can promise you, Solomon, like the branch secretary said in the Zoom meeting last night, senior management couldn't care less. One senior manager I was talking to today has a family member who's come down with Covid. He's got more things to worry about. As long as everyone's wearing a mask on the premises, they don't care about the design. It's a minor issue. Some flunky down the chain wants to make a hero of himself.'

'So, I'm getting a warning then?'

'Yep. don't sweat it. Take the warning, then appeal it. That's when we'll step in.'

'Okay.'

A year back, I would have been shaking in my boots at the thought of receiving a warning. But after being cooped up with Covid, I didn't care anymore. I could handle it.

I had an idea later that evening. I jumped on my computer and found a company that designed made to order masks. They didn't cost much, so I ordered seven masks. Each slightly different to the others. A simple design, just a bit different.

The masks were express posted to my home and were waiting at the steps by my front door the following day.

The next day at work I wore a white mask with one word typed in black bold capitals in the middle of the mask:

YOU

Stone saw the writing on my mask and smiled at me when I signed on. 'What are you up to now, Solly?' he asked with a grin on his face. The word 'YOU' meant nothing to Stone.

The next day I wore a different mask with the word:

ARE

The next day my mask had one letter:

A

The next day my mask had another letter:

C

Stone had gotten the gist of what was happening, and what was coming. He wasn't smiling anymore. Yet I was doing nothing wrong. Some of my co-workers had their favourite football team's colours as masks, others had colourful designs. I just had a couple of inoffensive words and a few letters. Stone couldn't do anything. Stone knew what I was up to, and he cut a dejected figure as he moped around the office. I had gotten to him. My co-workers saw what was happening and were enjoying the pantomime. They weren't too worried either about Stone's feelings.

The next day the letter on my mask was:

U

The next day:

N

One of my co-workers rang me during the day. He told me he'd overheard Stone on the phone having a whinge to his superiors about what I was up to. My co-worker could hear the manager on the other end of the line laughing at Stone, telling him to suck it up.

When the logistics manager from the larger office called me from the loudspeaker to come to the office for my warning the next morning, I stood at the side panel of the glass window. The logistics manager motioned me to come inside the office. There was already a seat waiting for me at the end of the table. I explained that because of social distancing Stone didn't like anyone in his office, preferring for everyone to stand outside. The logistics manager looked around the office. There was more than enough space for two people. Stone himself wasn't part of the warning so was in the lunchroom sitting by himself, having a cup of tea.

The logistics manager shrugged his shoulders and moved his chair a bit closer to the window where I was standing. He read out the two charges. I didn't offer a defence and pleaded guilty to both. He stated if it happened again there would be an escalation to a code of ethics inquiry. My mouth was dry when the manager spoke, and my legs were shaking the whole time. I had to hold onto the glass panel to steady myself. In two decades of faithful service to my employer, this was the first time I'd been written up. I was now officially a troublemaker with a permanent blemish on my record. The logistics manager finished up, rose from his seat and went to the photocopier to make a copy for me. He asked what the 'T' stood for on my mask. I regained my senses. 'Tenacity,' I told him. I reached into Stone's office, picked up the paperwork that was left on the edge of the desk, then slid the glass panel shut and returned to my station.

One of my co-workers must have rung the union to tell them what I'd done. At the next Zoom meeting the following week, the branch secretary explained the latest updates before he opened the meeting up to members to voice their concerns. He had a big cheesy smile on his hardened, gravelled face as he touched on another subject.

'Guys, I just want to offer my congratulations to one of our members. Solomon Baxter. I see he's listed at being at the meeting tonight. I know you can hear me, mate. I'll just give a run-down on what happened. You used your imagination, didn't you, Solomon? There's a saying we have here at the union. There's more than one way to skin a cat. Well done, Sol. Good for you.'

The branch secretary then explained to the hundred-plus members listening in my actions over the last week with the various masks I wore. After he finished, there were guffaws of laughter from him and the assistant secretary, who was also on the screen. The assistant secretary was banging his fist on the table, he was laughing so much. I had done it to piss off my manager, but it seemed to have struck a chord with the union organisers. I had reduced two hardened warriors to red-faced giggling gerties. The shit they must put up with. To them, Stone was just another dopey manager they had to deal with every day. It wasn't personal to them like it was to me. I didn't know how they did it, arguing with management all the time as they defended their members. But Covid and lockdowns were getting to everyone. Everyone was exhausted, so a bit of 'up yours' to management provoked an unexpected bout of laughter from my union comrades.

I knew now, I could handle someone like Stone. I felt a burden had been lifted. I had stomped on a pebble, and it felt good.

Grotto dell'uomo

The man looked to the backyard from his back door, pulled out his phone and dialled some numbers. The other end picked up.

'Sun Valley Produce.'

'Hi. Do you sell chickens?'

'We do. But because of Covid, we're just doing delivery at the moment. The shop is closed, but we can certainly deliver. Where do you live?'

The man replied that he lived in Medlow Bath. The clerk from the produce store said they delivered up his way twice a week.

'What type of chickens do you want?' the clerk asked.

'Surprise me,' the man replied. 'I'm just after some eggs.'

The clerk sold him two chickens, a couple of weeks from the point of lay. He also sold the man a plastic food bowl, some woodchips for the chickens to roost in the coop at night, and a bag of pellet food. The overall cost with the delivery fee came to 148 dollars. The man pulled out his credit card and read out the numbers.

***

The man had been cleaning underneath his house the last few days. It was cluttered with junk and needed a cleanout. His tools lay everywhere, and storage tubs, full of stuff he and his wife didn't want to throw out, were stacked untidily on top of each other.

Now it was the first day of the first week of his three weeks of holidays. He and his wife had borrowed money for their big trip overseas – 25 thousand to be exact. They were going to spend three weeks in the UK, travelling up and down the countryside like the millions of tourists that visited the UK every year. Catching trains, walking through London, gawking at statues, touring historic sites.

But then Covid struck, which shelved their UK trip. So they booked tickets to go to New Zealand instead, but then Jacinda Ardern closed down the country. The man decided to spend a week visiting his family in Queensland, but the states closed their borders. 'We'll do regional New South Wales,' the man told his wife, but that didn't happen either, because soon everyone in the country was placed under stay-at-home orders.

So, on the first day of their holidays, when he and his wife should have been holding hands, looking out the airplane window down to the Thames River before the wheels screeched on the tarmac and touched down at Heathrow Airport, the man was under his house, looking at the mess, trying not to be depressed. He had nothing to do for three weeks so he thought he may as well do a bit of cleaning. His wife in the lead-up to their big overseas trip had been learning Italian because she wanted to spend a couple of days in Rome. When the trip became a bust, she just sat on the couch watching telly, sadly swearing to herself in Italian. With the whole country shut down, with nowhere to go, and his wife cursing in another language, the man thought it was going to be a long three weeks.

So on the weekend before his holidays he decided to start building a man cave for himself under the house. He had heard that council was fast tracking any pick-ups left on the nature strips instead of having to wait the usual couple of months. So he went online and placed a pick-up collection order for the next week. On the Monday morning he connected his headphones to the bluetooth on his phone, turned on his music, put his overalls on and headed down the front steps.

It wasn't as bad a mess as he'd first thought when he'd tilted the door back, once he was under the house and his eyesight adjusted to the dark. The youngest of their children had left home a year back – they were empty-nesters now – and most of the contents of the tubs were really mementos: toys, clothes and keepsakes of their kids as they grew up over the years.

Some of the storage tubs were placed on top of an oak table that hadn't been useful for anything. The first thing the man did was clear the tubs off the table and drag it under a small window that was next to the door. There were some chairs behind the piles of tubs, that he'd scored off his grandmother when she died, and he slotted them in front of the table. Then he turned his attention to the shelves. He rearranged his tools, throwing away anything that looked rusted, broken or in a sad state of repair. The bigger stuff – some broken blinds, a rundown lawnmower, old petrol containers, empty paint tins, some old heaters and fans – went out front on a neat pile on the nature strip for council. He stacked the storage tubs on top of each other against the brick foundations near the door.

He had an Edwardian mantel piece that a neighbour had left on her nature strip for anyone to take if they wished, so the man, even though he didn't need a mantel piece at all, had dragged it home a few months back. He couldn't resist something free like that. Naturally, it had been thrown under the house with everything else and left to collect dust. He realised now that he was never going to use it for anything so he took the axe to it, and the splintered bits of wood ended up on the council pile on the nature strip.

He kept on stacking the tubs and gradually everything took shape. He was just about finished, when he squinted his eyes into the darkness and saw a roll of wire. He crouched forward, walked the width of the house and grabbed the wire, wondering should he keep it or throw it out on the nature strip for council to collect, when he thought of the coop at the back of the house. He hadn't kept chickens for ages. He'd built the coop himself and kept chickens on and off over the years as the boys grew up. He had enjoyed tending to the chickens. When they had started laying eggs, excitement filled the house. The man was just as happy as his children were. His boys, wearing their Wiggles gumboots, would almost run to the coop to collect the eggs.

The coop was at the back, wedged between the side and back fence of his neighbours. It had been a while since he'd given it a onceover. He walked to the coop and stood by the front gate. Everything looked alright. The wire fence was still standing, held upright by star pickets, the gate hadn't pulled away from the hinges, and the A-frame coop inside still looked sturdy. He had never gotten around to making a roof to fully keep the chickens safe, but the roll of wire he was holding in his hands would just about be enough to enclose the coop. The roll of wire inspired him to pull out his phone, call Sun Valley Produce, and ring through the order for a couple of chickens.

Then the man went back under the house and sat in the chair in front of his oak table. His man cave was finished. There was a power point above the table near the door so his wife had given him a spare kettle and a jar of tea bags, and he could charge his phone and plug in his headphones. He placed his cap on a nail sticking out of a beam to give his man cave a personal touch. He didn't really even know what men did in man caves. With lock-down and three weeks of holidays, he'd have plenty of time to figure it out. He reached across to the shelf and pulled a packet of tobacco from under a box of screws. He put the kettle on to boil, rolled a cigarette and when the tea had brewed, he took a sip of tea and lit up. His first cigarette in weeks. He took a deep satisfying drag, congratulating himself on a job well done.

Seconds later, his wife was thumping her shoes on the floorboards as she sat on the couch in the lounge room above him.

'Are you smoking?' she shrieked down to him. Her voice sounded like sheet metal tearing. She thumped the floorboards with her feet in anger. 'It stinks up here.'

He frantically blew away the smoke with his arms as he quickly stubbed out his cigarette on the floor with his foot.

'No, dear.'

He heard his wife mutter something in Italian as she stormed to the kitchen. *'Va' a farti fottore, bastardo.'*

Gosh, the man thought, her Italian is better than I realised. She had really been looking forward to our overseas trip.

The next day in his man cave he reached for his caulking gun, snipped open a tube of spare filler he'd found when he was cleaning up, and spent an hour filling the gaps between the floorboards above the table and chairs.

When he finished, he boiled the kettle, and when the tea brewed, he lit a cigarette, took a sip of his tea then blew the smoke from his cigarette towards the floorboards above him. His wife was sitting in the couch watching telly. The smoke hit the floorboards and didn't drift through the cracks. The filler had done its job. The smoke hovered above the man, going nowhere. There were no shrieks of displeasure or foot stomping from his wife. For the first time in a couple of days, the man smiled.

'*Bellissimo.*'

The chickens were delivered the following day. The driver pulled a hessian bag from the back of his truck and carried them up the side path while the man followed, grunting as he carried the bag of mulch, pellets and the water container. The driver opened the wire gate and turned the hessian bag upside down. Out popped a black Australorp and a white Leghorn. They were small and jittery as they adapted to their new surroundings. The man and the driver watched them as they scratched the dirt and pecked at the ground, looking for something to eat. The man ripped open the bag of pellets, and from the gate flicked a few handfuls onto the ground. The Australorp started putting her beak to the ground, the pellets quickly disappeared, and shortly after, the Leghorn followed.

'Give them a day or two to get used to their surroundings,' the driver told the man. He looked at the top of the enclosure.

'Maybe do something about the roof. Stop the foxes getting in,' he said.

'I plan to. I have the wire,' the man replied.

The man forgot about the wire, and completely forgot about the chickens until after dark. He rushed outside to find them roosting on top of the A-frame coop. They put up no resistance as he grabbed first the Australorp and put it inside, then did the same to the Leghorn and then latched them inside the coop for the night.

The next morning, just as dawn was breaking, he walked from the back door to the coop and opened the gate. He saw a possum with its baby on its back that had made its way from the open top into the enclosure and was eating the pellets that the chickens had left behind. He heard the chickens clucking inside the coop. They were awake and staring at him, waiting to be let out.

The man unlatched the door of the coop, and the two chickens cautiously crept outside. The man went to the bag of feed he kept in a plastic tub, flipped the lid, grabbed a handful of pellets and scattered them on the ground. They really do look like dinosaurs, the man thought as they pecked away at the ground. Their eyes, claws and mouth were giveaways. He snuck up behind the white Leghorn, picked it up and gently stroked the feathers of the startled bird. He made a list in his head of what food they would like besides the pellets, which would be boring for them after a while. Grated carrot, cheese, corn on the cob, watermelon. The man gently let the chicken back onto the ground and it darted away. The man rolled the bag of feed back into the tub, closed the gate, and then went under the house to his man cave for his first cigarette of the day. He heard his wife watching an episode of *House Hunters International.* A young couple were moving to Italy.

'Fotta, fottermi, minchia!'

The man was woken at night by the chickens causing a commotion. Something had disturbed them. He grabbed the torch by the back door and rushed to the coop. He was feeling a bit guilty because he hadn't managed to put the wire over the enclosure and secure them in properly. He opened the gate and shone the torch into the coop. The moment had passed, and all was calm. The chickens were snugly nestled on top of the wood shavings in the top part of the coop. The man saw the mother possum with its young on its back climbing a tree outside the wire fence, their eyes shining in the glare of the spotlight. That was probably what spooked them, the man thought. Relieved that the chickens were alright, he promised himself he'd get the wire roof done the next day. He closed the gate and went back to bed.

He forgot about the wire roof the next day. He'd been holed up in his man cave, smoking cigarettes, listening to his radio and foraging around in the storage tubs. Once in a while he'd make a racket and his wife would stomp like a horse from above and yell in Italian at him to keep quiet. He felt like swearing back at her, not worrying what language he spoke. Already lockdown was starting to do both their heads in. They had a whole house to themselves, but it still wasn't big enough.

He'd come across some old photos in one of the tubs when he was stacking them all together, so with nothing to do, he rummaged through them. One of the envelopes was crammed with snaps his mother had taken when he was young. Old, faded, glossy colour photos from the seventies. He pulled out one photo that caught his attention. It was of him when he was about ten years old, and on either side of him were his schoolmates Tony Guille and Nicholas Sinclair. He'd invited them over for the day and his mother had taken them all on a picnic for lunch. They'd been sitting on a bench seat at a park when his mother, sitting on the bench opposite, had taken their picture. The three of them were smiling at the camera, showing rows of white teeth; the wind had swept their hair across their foreheads and their skin was as white as vanilla ice cream. It was cold, so they had jumpers on. The man stared at the jumpers. His friend Tony had a brown jumper with V-shaped patterns running across the middle and Nicholas had a pale blue jumper with a white penguin on it. The man was wearing a green jumper that his mother had knitted for him for his birthday.

The man flipped the photo over. He could remember that picnic day like it was yesterday. After their lunch in the park they had climbed trees; once home again they had played cops and robbers in his backyard then listened to the footy match on the radio while they played billiards. His mother had written the date on the back – August 1977. The memory was especially strong because a couple of days later, he'd been in the lounge room watching television when his mother came in with tears in her eyes to tell him that Elvis Presley had died.

He found another roll of photos in the tub. Ones that the man had taken when he was a young adult. The first photo he pulled out was of a photo of an inner-city street. When he was in his early twenties, the man had roamed the streets of the town he lived in, with his camera around his neck, taking pictures of anything that appealed to him. He really just liked the architecture of the houses he walked past, so he stopped on the footpath and took pictures of them. He didn't know then how to properly describe the features he was seeing, but he now knew he was admiring the bluestone on the fronts of cottages, the wrought-iron gates on verandahs, the patterns of the brickworks, the elegant architecture of two-storey mansions and well-kept weatherboard cottages. The photo he held in his hand now was of a road, and in the middle of the road were tram tracks that the trams had stopped running along many years ago. That's why he'd taken the picture. The steel of the disused tram tracks glistened in the sun. He had adopted the habits of his mother so after he picked his photos up from the chemist, he'd written the month and the year on the back of every photo.

'December 1988,' he whispered to himself. He had a decent memory and was sure he'd taken the photo then. He flipped the picture and read his writing.

December 1988.

He pulled out a larger photograph sitting loosely in the tub. It was of his confirmation, when he was still at primary school. All the kids had congregated together on the netball court after the confirmation had taken place. Forty kids dressed in their best clothes, hunched together in three rows, staring at the camera. Despite his decent memory, the man couldn't remember the day of his confirmation at all, let alone having his photo taken to celebrate the event. He did remember, though, the Monday after his confirmation, that all the Italian kids had received wads of cash and the Anglo kids just got statues of Jesus that glowed in the dark and rosary beads. The man put his glasses on to see where his young self was in the photo. He was standing at the edge of the middle row, smiling his toothy grin. He remembered his mother had cut his hair in the lead-up to his confirmation, and his hair was combed to the side. Standing behind him in the photo was the priest. As the photo was being taken, the smiling priest had placed his hand on his arm.

'What the fuck!' the man exclaimed as he studied the picture more closely. He didn't remember that. He kept looking at the photograph of the priest with his hand on his arm, trying to will the memory to come back to him, but he couldn't. He looked at the photo for a long time, a million thoughts running through his head. Then he ripped the photo into pieces and burnt it with his cigarette lighter.

As his wife slept beside him that night, he lay in bed wide awake. He tried not to think of the photo of his confirmation. He was, instead, thinking how happy he'd been at the picnic when he was a child with his school mates, or when he was walking the streets on his own with a camera around his neck when he was older. He enjoyed life better when he was on his own, when he wasn't responsible to anyone, or he didn't have to justify his decisions to anyone. He'd had a great childhood, even if there was a creepy priest lurking around on the school grounds. Even now, he liked spending time on his own. He enjoyed his man cave. He wasn't answerable to anyone. As he lay on his side, staring at the wall in the darkness, he frowned. He had been unhappy long before Covid.

He was just about to fall asleep when he heard the chickens clucking. He'd forgotten again to enclose the roof. He'd been cooped up himself in his man cave, reminiscing over old photos, thinking, trying to remember things, secretly smoking his cigarettes, upsetting his wife with the noises he made. The mother possum must be foraging for food with her young in the coop again, he thought. His wife continued to snore away, and the clucking of the chickens died down. He promised himself that, tomorrow, he'd finish the roof of the coop. He closed his eyes and went to sleep.

The next morning, he stood at the gate of the enclosure. The mother possum and its child were lying near the door. Both their heads had been ripped off. The baby possum was still clinging onto its mother, its claws embedded in her back. They were lying in a clotted pool of their own blood.

The A-frame coop had been torn apart. There were broken pieces of wood flung about, and in the bottom floor of the battered coop, bunched together and covered in dirt, lay the two chickens. They looked like they were sleeping, but they were dead. The eyes of the Australorp were open but lifeless, and the Leghorn had scratches all across her white face.

He closed the gate, went down the side path and under his house to his man cave. He sat still in his chair, with his head in his hands, for several minutes. Then he pulled out his pouch of tobacco and he smoked cigarette after cigarette, not caring if his wife could smell the smoke above him. He turned the radio up so she couldn't hear him crying. After an hour of sitting in his chair, he walked to the driveway and drove to the supermarket. He bought two dozen eggs, came back home and dropped the cartons on the table in his man cave. He opened one of the cartons and grabbed two eggs, then walked through the back door into his house. His wife was in the kitchen, still in her dressing gown, making her morning coffee. She spotted the two eggs in his hand.

The man saw her smile. A slight smile. Warmth in her eyes. He hadn't seen that for a while. 'They're finally laying?' she asked him.

'They're finally laying, honey,' he replied. The man kissed his wife on the cheek; she smiled a wider smile, then he went to put the eggs in the fridge.

The motorbike and the hill

The man rolled the bike out from under the house and wheeled it to the nature strip. It was Friday morning and it was the last few days before daylight saving kicked in, so it had been light outside for a while. Cockatoos were screeching to the sky while nestled nearby in the tall trees that shadowed the side of his house. He checked the petrol and the oil. He had given the bike a bit of a clean the night before and it had come up trumps. The chrome sparkled in the morning sun; the paint on the petrol tank and the oil cover that was sixty years old looked as if it was painted on yesterday.

He didn't know why, when he was in his fifties, he still felt the need to show his bike off a little bit. His bones creaked, his body always ached and there was grey in his hair. At this age he should be a contented man, yet his insecurities were still high, and he still felt he needed the approval of others. He'd been this way since he was a kid. He wondered if others the same age felt the same way, but he doubted it. He had always felt different than other people. Ever since he was a kid, he never knew what normal was. He just knew he didn't possess it. As he grew older, he realised the key to fitting in was just to hide in plain sight. Hide your shyness. Pretend to understand everything. Bluff your way through life. Keep your mouth shut, laugh along with everyone else. Disguise your pain with humour. Use alcohol to hide your loneliness. Bluff your way through marriage and parenthood. Try to learn from your mistakes. Keep failing, but don't give up.

Though he didn't do it that often, he liked showing the bike off. He was proud of it. The bike really was an eye-catching motorcycle. A good-looking relic from another age that you don't see much of anymore. The chrome hadn't rusted at all over the years, the black rubber on the pegs and the handlebars still looked new, and the two tones of blue paint on the petrol tank and cover plates were a masterpiece of art. And the sound it made was a sound like no other bike he had ever heard. The mufflers produced a thick, deep rumbling sound that caused people in the street to pause and turn, and wonder what the approaching noise was when he rode around town.

He thought after thirty years of owning an old British bike, he would know a thing or two about mechanics, but he was none the wiser about the workings of the bike than when he first bought it all those years back when he was nineteen. It added to his insecurities. Surely with such a vintage piece of machinery in your possession, you should know a little bit about bikes. He knew he should, but he didn't.

But he decided a couple of days back to ride the bike to work, give it a spin, and show it off to his workmates. It was his last day of work for a while.

He was on holidays for six weeks and had been in a good mood for days. A couple of his co-workers had done up some old bikes over the years in their garages and were riding them to work. Some of his workmates knew about his Norton, and every once in a while asked him how it was going. The last time he had ridden it to work was about eight years ago, so to most of his colleagues, it was a distant memory.

The bike wasn't registered, but the man wasn't too worried. It was only a three-kilometre ride to work. He hadn't returned the number plate to the RMS when the rego expired a few years back, and it was still screwed at the back under the taillight, so for all intents and purposes, the bike looked like it was registered. He was only travelling on the highway for a few hundred metres before turning off at the hospital lights towards North Katoomba. He'd be a bit stiff and unlucky if a cop car ended up behind him and he was collared for riding an unregistered vehicle.

So after his morning shower and after he gently pecked his still sleeping wife on her cheek, he ran down the front steps, went under the house and wheeled the bike onto the nature strip. He jumped on the bike, put on his helmet, turned on the ignition, flicked the petrol switch, hopped on the foot pedals and came down hard with all his weight on the kick-starter.

Boom, boom, boom, boom, the mufflers went. He massaged the throttle until it was warmed up, then he released the throttle and let it idle.

Boom, boom, boom. It was purring, a deep, satisfying, rumbling sound.

The man clicked his bike into gear, let out the clutch and rode off the nature strip and up the street.

There were no cops to worry about on the stretch of highway as the bike hummed along with the other morning traffic. The bike idled perfectly as the man waited for the green arrow at the highway turnoff, and the drum brakes held as he went down the steep showground hill. He turned left onto Orient Street, then right at Barton, and headed towards the office.

The bike broke down at the crossroad intersection just as he was turning into the street of his work. It made a weak gurgling noise then just died on him. The lights went off and he lost power. He had no choice but to pull in the clutch and roll the bike the last one hundred metres. He felt as meek as a mouse as he rolled the bike down the driveway at his work. There was no 'whoa' or 'wow' from his workmates. There was no nothing. Because the bike had broken down, no one had heard him arrive. He felt embarrassed that the bike had conked out on him so he pushed it behind the back of the shed so no one would see it. He was too deflated to even bother to see what was wrong with it. It might have been something simple like a loose battery connection. The man couldn't be bothered. He was embarrassed. He just wanted to show it to some workmates, but you can't show it to anyone when you can't start the thing.

The man parked the bike behind the shed where the broken pallets and the bins were, leant it against the building, went to pull the key out of it, and thought, *Why bother? Who would steal this piece of shit?* He was angry. He spat on the petrol tank; he kicked the tyres. He cursed.

'The fucking fucker's fucked,' he shouted to himself.

He wondered as the day wore on, as he sat in front of his computer at his desk, how was he going to get the bike home? It was the last day before the school holidays began, it was the Labour Day weekend, so everyone was giving themselves an early mark and going away. He had rung several towing firms over the course of the day but no one had answered. He couldn't blame them. The man was going away as well. He had booked a holiday up the north coast with his family and was leaving tomorrow morning. He wasn't a member of the NRMA: money had been tight the last few months. His wife had recently resigned from her job, they were back to being a single income family and they'd been putting aside every cent they could spare for their holiday for months. The man felt it was an indulgent luxury to spend two hundred dollars to have a bike towed three kilometres. It was easy money for the tow-truck drivers but easy money or not, it didn't make them feel inclined to pick up their phones when he rang. He was more upset that in his sixth decade of life, he didn't have a mate who owned a ute that he could make a quick phone call to, a mate who would help him throw the bike on the back of the ute, then receive a slab of beer in appreciation when it was dropped off outside his house. He couldn't leave the bike parked out the back for six weeks. Other companies in the building block had access to the back of the building as well. It dawned on him as the afternoon wore on that as the towing companies didn't pick up their phones, he was on his own with this one. His stomach sank at the realisation. He would have to push the bike home. It was his only solution. He thought of the showground hill near the hospital by the highway. It was steep, like a mountain from the Himalayas. But what choice did he have?

He waited until after his co-workers had all left. They had all snuck out a bit earlier, wanting to make the most of the long weekend. That suited him. He didn't want them to see him pushing his bike out from the back of the building. He didn't want them to see him wheeling his broken-down bike back home. When he knew he was the last worker remaining in the building, he logged out of his computer, shoved his helmet in his locker, turned the lights off in the building, set the alarm by the roller door, exited the main entrance and walked to the back of the building.

He grabbed the bike by the handlebars, backed it past the pallets and the bins, straightened the bike up then wheeled it down the side to the front driveway.

He had broken the trip into three parts. The first part was getting to the bottom of the hill near the highway. There were a couple of small inclines on the road, but he didn't think they would present too much of a problem. It was a nice stretch of road. The second would be the most daunting, easily the hardest bit of the trip. Wheeling the bike up the steep showground hill. The third would be the easiest. Once he made it up the hill, he would be going down the mountains. It was literally downhill all the way from there to his home.

He grunted and took a deep breath, leant forward and started to push the bike from the driveway along the footpath. He had given himself ten minutes to get to the bottom of the showground hill. The houses came and went as he pushed the bike forwards. It sure was a bonus, the flat footpath. Sometimes he almost broke into a canter. The weight and momentum of the bike carried him along. He passed a woman feeding some parrots on her front balcony. He nodded to a man he passed in another house who was watering his garden in his front yard. He saw small chunks of wood that had fallen off trucks lying in the gutters with the other normal rubbish and he saw a dead galah face down on the ground, its feathers spread out on the grass.

It wasn't the first time he had pushed the bike a long distance. When he was young and living interstate, he had pushed the bike from his parents' home to the flat he had just moved into, which was five kilometres away. He remembered he didn't have a licence and was worried about getting caught by the cops. He wanted the bike at his flat, was in a hurry, and was too stubborn to wait for his father to help him figure out how he was going to get it there. So, he pushed the bike five kilometres. It was flat all the way, no steep hills to worry about. He didn't know why he didn't just wait for his father to finish what he was doing. The man tried to think, as he pushed the bike past the houses along the nature strip, what it was exactly that his father was held up with. It was so long ago. Then the man remembered. It was visitors. Some friends had popped over unexpectedly, and his father had joined them at the table for a cup of tea, a chat and a catch-up.

The man felt like an idiot. How old had he been back then? Nineteen? Twenty maybe. Just a boy, really. He was too stubborn to wait for the visitors to leave, so he wheeled the bike over four suburbs, pushing the same bike he was pushing now, just to prove a point. He had long forgotten what point he was trying to prove to his father. Was he jealous that his father was spending time with other people? His father was healthy then, working at the casino. The man remembered he did ride the bike for a little bit when he was wheeling it to his flat. The temptation was too much. He rode the bike along a straight stretch of road that ran parallel to the beach. His concerns for getting caught by the police, though, were well founded. He stopped riding the bike, started pushing it again, turned a corner and there was a cop on a patrol bike, hiding behind a huge boulder on the Currumbin Beach foreshore. They nodded to each other as he rolled the bike by. If he had ridden past, the cop would have surely got the sirens going, chased him, pulled him over, done him for unlicensed driving as well as an unregistered vehicle. He would have had a pile of fines to pay.

The man took a break from pushing the bike along the nature strip. It might have been okay pushing 150-odd kilograms of English machinery when you were in your late teens, but there wasn't much joy doing it when you're in your mid-fifties. He was out of breath, his back ached, his shoulders tingled and the muscles in his arms were drained of all their strength. He pulled a bottle of water from his pocket, rested the bike against the wire fence in front of a red-brick commission house and took a few deep gulps. Cars drove past him on the road, some drivers giving him a side glance, wondering what he was up to. Others just zipped past him, full of indifference, eager to get to where they were going. As he rested and caught his breath, he figured he was halfway done on the first leg of his trip. He could see the hill over the roofs of houses in the distance. The showground oval and the hospital were behind the hill. He could see an ambulance in slowly making its way to the emergency ward. The hill was approaching. It wasn't far away. It looked steep, and it dominated the landscape. He took some deep breaths, picked his bike up, and resumed pushing it along the footpath.

He had never argued with his father. They got along very well. Even during his teenage years when they were all cramped in a small house, he couldn't remember bluing that much with the old man. They were more mates than father and son. They went on walks along the beach together; they rode pushbikes around the neighbourhood they lived in. When his father got drunk at the golf course or at the local pubs, the man would hop in the family car and pick him up. He played squash with his father when he was a boy and his old man taught him how to drive. They went to movies together, watched the cricket on the telly, swapped comic magazines they liked. The man could only remember his father being angry with him once when he was younger. He had taken the family radio to the beach to listen to music as he lay on a towel, basking in the sun. A rogue wave broke on the shore and drenched everyone lying on the sand. The radio was ruined. His father was angry at him. That was the only time he remembered his father losing his temper.

Then the man left home, moved interstate, married, started a family. When his father was 47, he became ill with Crohn's disease. His father put up with it for 18 years, being sick, being in and out of hospital, being operated on. His father must have thought, *I don't need this shit. Enough's enough.* So he wrote some goodbye notes, got stuck into a bottle of red wine in his bedroom when his wife was out, took some pills and died of a drug overdose.

The man reached the intersection that led to the hill. It wasn't far away now. 100 metres, 150 at the most. He grunted, dug in his heels, turned the wheel of the bike left and continued along the footpath.

It was a bit of a shock, getting a phone call out of the blue. His brother had rung him. 'Dad died,' was all his brother had said. You think they'll live forever. Even with his old man being sick for so long, it was inconceivable to him that any of his parents would die. The man was either drunk or hungover pretty much every day for a month after his father died, using alcohol to absorb the grief. Hearing well-wishers tell him at the funeral, 'It was the best thing that ever happened to him,' was a bit hard to take. He knew they meant no harm. His father had been sick for so long. He just wasn't ready to hear it.

The man made it to the bottom of the hill. The first bit was over. He rested the bike on the stand as he had a rest. He looked up the hill. He knew how Edmund Hillary and Tenzing Norgay felt when they were just about to climb Mt Everest. The hill loomed large, steep and menacing. He knew he was going to struggle. The only strategy he could think of was, just take one step at a time. That's the best he could come up with. That's all he had. If it was too much, he'd have to drop the bike, then pick it up, roll it back down the hill and hide it somewhere. That sounded more exhausting than pushing the bike up the hill. He reckoned the hill was only fifty metres long before it flattened out up the top. Fifty metres equalled roughly fifty steps. The yellow rugby league goal posts on the showground oval on his left stood out against the freshly mown and lush green grass. The grandstand stood by the middle of the oval, and next to that was the asphalted carpark. Between the grandstand and the ground was a trotting track. A gust of wind picked up some sand from the track and blew it across the oval. There was a hive of activity in the canteen under the grandstand in the club rooms. A volunteer was chalking the try line at the other end of the ground. The local team must be hosting some finals action on the weekend. His youngest son had played league in his primary school years. The man could remember sitting with his wife in the grandstand, watching their son play for the junior teams.

He took some last deep breaths for the task ahead, flicked the bike off the stand and took the first steps up the hill.

His hand hovered over the front brake on the right of the handlebars as he pushed the bike forwards, in case he had to quickly squeeze the brake when he needed to rest. He made the first ten steps okay before it became too much for him. He held the bike upright, his hand squeezing the front brake as he caught his breath. Then he thought, *let's go,* and pushed the bike a bit further up the hill. He made another five steps before he stopped again. The top of the hill didn't look any closer than when he first started. He knew he had made a start because the vibrations from the trucks thundering past the highway above him became stronger. He made another five steps then stopped again. *Fuck,* he thought, grimacing in pain. *I'm going to fucking die of a fucking heart attack pushing a fucking motorbike up a fucking hill.* He leant the bike against himself, his hand clutching the front brake lever. Then he lurched forwards, let go of the lever and made another five steps. It was murder. Sweat ran down the side of his face. He took another five steps. There were two telegraph poles on the hill by the footpath. He passed the first telegraph pole. A milestone. When he stopped and looked down, he laughed. It didn't look steep at all and he had only travelled twenty metres or so. All that effort and toil for such a short distance. He looked up at how much he had to go. He stopped laughing. A minute later, after another pause, he had cause for celebration. He was halfway up the hill. He took another couple of steps. Now he was more than halfway. He thought of his father, being sick for so long, the courage he had in the end. The man used the suffering his father endured for so long to summon extra strength and continue onwards. He started to shake from pushing, he was red-faced, his cheeks were puffing in and out and his mouth was dry. He was getting funny looks from cars passing by. Look at this fuckwit, they must have been thinking. But he was going to make it. He kept his hand above the brake lever the whole time as he took one step, then another, and then another. He passed the other telegraph pole and kept on going. He could feel blood form above his top lip, his head was aching and the muscles in his legs were killing him. But with a final heave the front tyre levelled out. He had reached the top of the hill. He pushed the bike one last time then rested it against the wire fence that ran along the showground. His clothes were saturated with sweat, he was hunched over, and he could barely stand. He was sucking in deep breaths, too exhausted to celebrate, but he had done it. He looked down to the bottom of the hill. It didn't look that steep now he was at the top. He felt proud of what he'd achieved. He hadn't keeled over from a heart attack. He hadn't died. He had forgotten about the bottle of water he had in his back pocket. The bottle was crinkled and crushed but it didn't stop him from greedily guzzling down the few mouthfuls that were left.

He pulled the bike towards him and pushed it a few steps further. He was on a downward trajectory; the slope down the mountains beckoned. The bike started to go faster, the man hopped on his motorcycle and he paddled his feet like Fred Flintstone. He glided past the hospital and hugged the shoulder of the road as he rolled down the highway. He used the back and front brakes as he turned off the highway into his street. He rolled down the hill and a minute later he was in the driveway of his house.

He pushed the bike one last time past the driveway to the door that led under the house. Despite his accomplishment of pushing the bike all the way from his work, he was sick of owning an old English bike. For a minute the man contemplated selling it. It just sat under the house gathering dust. He did make one decision, though. He would never push the bike like he'd just done ever again as long as he lived. This was the last time.

Just before he went to push the bike under the house, for no reason other than idle curiosity, he turned the ignition on. There was a charge on the ammeter display on top of the light. He frowned. There hadn't been a charge on the ammeter when it broke down this morning. He put the bike on its stand, turned the petrol tap on, stood on the bike, placed his foot on top of the kickstarter and brought it down.

Boom, boom, boom, boom. The bike roared into life. Whatever ailment that troubled the bike in the morning had been forgotten. The bike hummed like an angel singing from the clouds. It didn't miss a beat.

What the fuck, the man thought. He yelled at the bike, 'What trickery are you playing here?'

He turned off the bike. He stood next to it, still covered in sweat, still with every muscle aching. The bike had made a fool of him. He wanted to push the bike to the ground, stomp on it a few times, then light a rag with petrol, throw it in the petrol tank and burn the fucking thing to the ground. Then the man smiled. Then he started laughing. He couldn't stop. He couldn't remember the last time he laughed so hard. What a great start to his holidays.

The man was still laughing to himself as he flicked up the stand and rolled his bike underneath the house.

The belonging mind

I was sitting in the waiting room of my local clinic. I'd turned up early, hopeful of a quick visit but, as always, my doctor was running late. I'd been waiting over half an hour, and I was bored and irritable. My phone had gone flat, which amplified my annoyance. I absentmindedly flicked through some wilted *National Geographic* magazines on the table in front of me. I saw a current edition of the local newspaper resting on an empty chair near me, so with nothing else to do I stretched my arm out and grabbed it. I unfolded the paper and turned the pages. I glossed over the features and articles, the classifieds, then hit the public notices at the back of the paper. One of the ads near the bottom of the page caught my eye. It was square shaped, typed in bold and only ran for three lines. The first two read:

> **Alien life form seeks bodyguard.**
> **Princess K.**

The third line was a mobile phone number.

I read the ad again. A joke surely? A misprint that went through production unnoticed, maybe. While I waited to be called in by my doctor, I indulged myself. I was unemployed and had been out of work for weeks, but I might actually be qualified for this bodyguard position. I'd been training in martial arts since I was a child and had held my black belt for years. I had competed in competitions around the world, been ranked in the top fifty when I was at my peak in my twenties, and while I was never good enough to reach any finals in any of the tournaments I'd entered, I had a lot of fun. I went to places I would never have dreamed of, formed strong friendships with many of my opponents, and even though my competing days were now behind me, I was still fit and strong. There wasn't an ounce of fat on me. I was a life member of my local martial arts centre and still trained there several times a month. As my last job placement was six weeks back, things were beginning to look grim. I read the ad again. I could apply for it if it wasn't so preposterous. Alien life form? What did that even mean? I didn't understand.

'Nicholas?'

My doctor was at the front door of her consulting room, calling my name. By the puzzled look on her face, she had called my name more than once. I looked around the waiting room. It was empty. The patients that I had been sitting with had gone. How long had I been reading the paper for? It felt like it was for only a minute. I seemed to have been in a trance over this alien life form advertisement. Embarrassed, I jumped from my seat, folded the newspaper in half and put it in my coat pocket, and walked towards the doctor.

I held off as long as I could, but when I couldn't get to sleep and I kept rolling over and over in my bed, my brain unable to rid itself of curiosity and intrigue, I caved.

I turned on the lamp, reached for my phone on my bedside table and opened the newspaper.

I didn't really know what to say. It was such an outlandish ad, but I was broke, and there might be some money in it. What did I have to lose? In the end I sent a simple message.

Interested in the position advertised. Nicholas.

A message was fired back immediately.

Meet me tomorrow at the Burger Palace. 11am. Princess K.

Finally, I was able to sleep.

I walked through the doors to a near-empty restaurant just before eleven. There were two men in black suits that I passed, sitting at a booth, enjoying an early lunch.

I saw someone sitting alone in another booth on their own at the back of the restaurant. I made my way over.

It was a woman. She looked nervous at the sound of my approaching footsteps. Slim looking, she had golden hair going down to her waist. She had the bluest eyes I had ever seen. They were the colour of the deepest Nordic lake. She had a sprinkling of freckles spread across her nose and cheeks, and her lips were perfectly formed. My legs turned to jelly. Some alien life form this turned out to be.

'Nicholas?' she asked me. There was a half-smile, infectious and alluring. Her round blue eyes offered warmth and comfort.

'Princess K?'

I sat opposite her in the booth.

There was a plate of finished food in front of her.

'Sorry, I was hungry,' Princess K told me after she saw my eyes glance down at the plate. She poured me a glass of water and rested it in front of me. The accent was a rehearsed English, maybe. A mixture of German or French? I couldn't tell.

'The first question people usually ask me is,' Princess K began, 'are you an actual alien?'

'Sorry to interrupt,' I said to her. 'Do you hear those noises?' I tilted my head. I could hear voices, soft and muffled, coming from somewhere.

'What noises?'

'I can hear people whispering.' It sounded like there were people around us talking. I turned around but only saw the early lunch-goers I'd passed on my way in, but they were halfway through their meals and were eating in silence. They were too far away anyway for me to hear their conversation. I shrugged my shoulders, dismissed my suspicions and turned and leant back in the booth. Our eyes locked on each other just a second. A second longer than they should have with someone you've just met.

'Sorry, did you say you were an alien? I didn't read the ad properly.'

We laughed. It broke the ice. Princess K explained that she was, indeed, an alien and was stuck on earth indefinitely. I asked how many applicants she received from her ad. 'Just the one,' she said. 'You. Most people think the ad is a joke.' Princess K told me she needed protection from 'government types' who were after her. I told her I could be a bodyguard, that I'd never been one before, but I explained my years of martial arts training. She seemed impressed and nodded approvingly.

'Can you start now?' she asked.

'Why? Do you need protecting now?'

'As a matter of fact, I do.' Her eyes darted to my left.

I looked over my shoulder. The two men in suits that had been dining when I entered had waited for their cronies to arrive, and now there were four of them. They were standing behind me and were staring at Princess K. One of them still had his serviette tucked into his shirt while another was wiping crumbs from his mouth. Their reinforcements were just as silent and brooding as they glared at Princess K.

'Government types?' I turned back and asked her. She nodded again.

'Okay,' I said.

I stood up and the one on the left took a swing at me. I blocked his arm and punched him in the stomach. I heard his ribs crack and he grunted in pain. I stomped on the toes of the next one and punched him in the nose, his blood splattering on the floor. The third one didn't have time to flex his muscles before I delivered a roundhouse kick that sent him sprawling over the table behind him. I wasn't worried about subtlety with the fourth agent as he lunged at me with a chair above his head, so

I kicked him right between his legs. The chair fell to his side, forgotten, as he slumped on his knees, red-faced and groaning. I turned to Princess K. The moment it took to put all four away was exhilarating. I was smiling, full of adrenalin.

'Did I pass the audition?' I asked her.

I saw a sleek black sedan screech to a halt outside the restaurant. More agents ran from the car. Princess K grabbed my hand, and we raced through the kitchen and out the rear of the restaurant. We sprinted through the back streets and laneways of the city, running on concrete, running past buildings and parking lots. We ran until we could run no more, and only stopped when we thought we were out of reach of our pursuers.

Princess K grabbed hold of me and pushed me against the wire fence of a construction lot.

'In answer to your earlier question,' she said, smiling, her eyes full of intimate anticipation, 'Yes, you passed the audition.' She planted her lips on mine and we kissed. Her lips were warm and moist, and tasted of caramel and icing sugar. My knees began to buckle. My eyes were still closed when she pulled away from me.

'I have to go. I have to be somewhere,' Princess K said.

'Take me with you?' I said to her. 'I've got nowhere to be.'

She reached into her pocket and handed me a watch. It resembled a Dick Tracy watch I had worn when I was a kid. Except of course, it wasn't. While there was a small clock at the top end like there was with the original, the other part contained a small black screen. Something told me that the black screen was more advanced than the two-way radio Dick Tracy used to help foil his enemies.

I lifted my arm and Princess K rolled up my sleeve and wrapped it around my wrist.

'Anytime I need help, I'll contact you through this watch. No one can track it. It's just for you and me.'

She gently held my cheeks in her hands, closed her eyes, and kissed me one last time. Then her hands fell away, and without looking at me she ran down a side street and was gone.

The watch vibrated. I looked down. There was already a message on the screen.

I'll be in touch. K.

I looked around to see if the coast was clear. I didn't see any agents looming about. I put my hands in my pockets and headed home.

I waited three days until I heard from Princess K again. I'd been pining for her since the minute she disappeared. There were three thousand dollars in my account the day after we met. I don't know how she knew my bank details, but I knew it was from her. That was my payment. That was my fee. I spent my time walking around the city, drinking my booze in brown paper bags, searching for Princess K. The buildings, the skylines and the sun didn't look the same. I lost my appetite and stopped eating.

I'd been after some quick cash to tide me over, but I wasn't worried about money anymore. Sometimes you make bigger discoveries when you're looking for something else.

I was at home, lying on the sheets of my bed, empty bottles at my feet, when my watch buzzed. I hadn't taken the watch off my wrist since Princess K had put it there. A message came through.

Nicky, I need your help. The hardware store near the school at Rockley Parade. Hurry please.

I sprinted down the stairs of my flat, jumped in my car and headed downtown. There was a traffic jam at the outskirts of town. I banged my fist on the steering wheel in frustration, but there was nothing I could do. There were roadworks that were finishing up, and I was late getting to Rockley Parade. I saw Princess K in a vacant lot next to the hardware store, standing next to rubbish bins, her back against the wall, surrounded by 'government types'. I sped the car up and caught the agents by surprise. A couple of them crashed and bumped across the top of my bonnet before disappearing in front of the radiator.

I pinned a couple more agents when I rammed the car against a brick wall, then jumped out of the car as the other agents turned their attention to me. It didn't take long to finish off the rest of them.

I ran across the asphalt and reached Princess K.

'Sorry I'm late,' I told her. 'There was traffic.' She hugged me tightly. I didn't need much incentive to hug her back. We stepped over the bodies of the agents. They were still, covered in blood – there was no coming back for any of them. We walked arm in arm to the entrance of the vacant lot.

'What happened?' I asked her.

'I was in Entermann's donut shop, of all places,' she began. 'One of their patrol cars driving past saw me, chased me down the street. I thought I could outrun them, but more turned up and they cornered me. I thought I could handle them on my own; in the end there were too many of them. So I got in touch with you, and here we are.'

'Why are they after you?'

'Because I'm different but look the same. They want me so they can operate on me, see what I look like when they open me up. I've been evading them my whole time on this planet.'

She turned and faced me; her hands snaked around my waist. I wanted to ask her more questions. Was she the only one? How long she had been on Earth? Why was she even here? I didn't get the chance. We kissed for the second time on the footpath outside the vacant lot. A longer kiss than the first and I didn't want it to end. I ran my fingers through her long hair as she lifted my top from my trousers and spread her hands along my back. Then someone drove past and honked their horn at us. Princess K pulled away from me at the interruption, biting her bottom lip as she looked at me.

'It's okay,' I told her. 'I know what's going to happen. You can't stay. You have to go. I understand.'

'I'm always on the run. I hate it.' She kissed me again, then with both her thumbs she closed my eyelids. The most romantic act anyone has ever done to me. When I opened them a couple of seconds later she was gone. I heard sirens in the distance. Our actions hadn't gone unnoticed. I had to move.

But I wasn't letting her get away so easily this time. I ran to my car. Steam hissed from the radiator grille from banging into the wall when I killed the agents, but I managed to start it. I drove up lanes, one-way streets, looking, searching. I thought I saw a fleeting glimpse of the back of someone with long blonde hair disappear into a unit block next to a shopping complex. By the time I did a U-turn and reached the unit block, there was no sign of Princess K. I drove off, not knowing if I imagined seeing her or not.

I was lying on my bed, staring at the ceiling, trying to understand the confusion I felt. How empty your life feels when someone new comes into it. How can it happen so quickly? Is it love you feel? Is it obsession? I couldn't sleep. It was after two in the morning when my watch flashed.

Nicky?

Are you okay, Princess? Do you need help? I messaged back.

I'm alright. I don't need any help. Are you doing anything?

Nothing.

Come to my place.

Okay. Where do you live?

You know where I live. You saw when you followed me earlier.

Ten minutes later I parked the car out front of the unit block by the shopping centre and leapt up the steps of the complex two at a time. There was one unit where all the lights were on. I reached the third floor and saw the light glowing under the front door. I caught my breath, feeling tense and nervous, and just as I was about to knock, the door opened slightly. I pushed the door open and made my way in.

Later on, when we were sitting on the edge of her bed in her bedroom, and I was kissing her neck, I whispered to her that I wanted to walk with her through fields of flowering tulips, holding hands, the sun beaming on us as I promised her the world.

'Oh, Nicky,' Princess K sighed.

We hung out together. At night when everyone was asleep, we'd go to the small common courtyard out the back. I bought a hammock from the hardware shop and set it up in the middle of the yard. Other unit dwellers used it during the day. There were always cigarette butts and empty bottles of alcohol lying on the ground by the hammock. It didn't bother us. It was always free at night when we wanted it. We would lie and swing in it together, staring at the moon as I ran my fingers through her golden hair. When the sky was clear, I would point to the stars,

'Is it that one?' I would ask her. 'Is that where you're from?'

'No Nicky.'

Then I would randomly point to another star.

'What about that one?'

'Not even close, my darling.'

If she felt homesick as we made our way back up to her unit, I'd pluck flowers from the neighbours' gardens in the front yards and bundle them up with string into a bouquet to cheer her up.

Inside, we played hide and seek and used our Dick Tracy watches to send clues to see if we could find each other. It was a small flat, but we still found imaginative places to hide. The game usually ended with us laughing when our hiding spot was revealed, then one of us would chase after the other as we ran to the bedroom. The neighbours downstairs would have hated our stomping on the floors as we raced through the rooms.

One night we snuck out to a late-night movie screening. So no one could see us we snuck in just as the feature started and the lights had dimmed, and sat in the back seats of the theatre. There weren't many cinema-goers there, we had the whole back row to ourselves. We laughed when we got home. We couldn't recall a single scene from the film.

I walked into the bedroom with a kitchen knife one night and placed it in Princess K's hand. I rolled up my sleeve. I told her what I wanted done.

'It will hurt, Nicky. It will bleed and scar.'

'I know that. Get cracking, Princess.'

She took the handle of the knife and with precision

and care, she cut into my skin with the tip of the blade and carved the letter K into my forearm. I felt no pain at all, and when she finished, Princess K looked at me, stuck her tongue out and licked the blood that ran down my arm.

'My beautiful Princess.'

Another night we went to a nightclub called Rafters on the edge of the city. The setting was sparse industrial chic. Metal, welded steel, gleaming chrome, car panels and street signs on the walls. We sat at a table under the dim light at the back, together, sipping on our cocktails as we watched the clubbers on the dance floor, jammed together, fuelled by drugs, sweating to the rhythm of the thumping music as the strobe light flashed. We held hands under the table the whole time, silent, watching as the dance floor became more crowded. There was a large mirror above the bar. I looked at my reflection. The lights made me look ten years younger, but it wasn't the light that had turned me back to my twenties. It was because of the woman sitting next to me. Princess K followed my gaze. Our eyes locked and we stared at each other in the large mirror. For seconds, though it seemed an eternity. We squeezed our hands tighter. There was no need for any conversation. Our eyes said it all.

When Princess K was sleeping during the day, I'd stare out the windows onto the street, seeing if any patrol cars or agents were lurking about. I'd go to the supermarket and get food and cook her breakfast and have dinner ready for when she was hungry. Her metabolism was off the charts. For someone so thin, her appetite dwarfed mine.

Sometimes I could hear the same quiet and foggy whispers that I heard when I first met Princess K in the booth at the restaurant, but I couldn't figure out where they came from. I would hear them while I was lying next to Princess K in bed, or when I was staring out the windows. I could never make out what they were saying. In the end, I gave up thinking about them. I didn't want any distractions to get in the way of our happiness.

We were together a fortnight, then one morning as we were lying in bed, there was an ominous tone about the suddenness of the car that pulled up outside. I jumped to the window and peered through the blinds. I saw agents spilling out of the car.

'It's them, isn't it?' Princess K asked with resignation and dread in her voice.

'They've found us.'

We raced to the front door, went out and held on to the railing in the foyer as we looked down the stairwell. This time they had taken no chances. There were too many of them. I counted eight at least, and four were already running in single file up the flight of stairs. I heard another car screech to a halt outside.

'Princess,' I said to her. 'If we're gonna get out of here, we have to get to the roof.' We heard the sounds of helicopters from above. Our eyes widened with fear. We couldn't use the roof to make our escape.

We rushed back inside the unit and locked the door.

In seconds there was thumping at the door. I could hear the agents taking turns running and banging into it. The hinges would soon buckle. They would be inside within minutes.

We opened the blinds of the bedroom window and looked outside. There were agents on the footpath looking up at us. We were surrounded. The wood on the door was beginning to splinter from the agents' continued attacks. It wouldn't be long now. I turned to Princess K. I had tears running down my face.

'I'm sorry, Princess K,' I wailed. 'I couldn't protect you. I wasn't the man you needed me to be. I'm sorry.'

'Never ever say sorry to me, Nicky. There is one thing you can do, my darling, if you want me to live.'

'What are you waiting for?'

She wrapped my arms around me and looked into my eyes. The agents were nearly through, and they would soon have their greedy clutches on Princess K.

'There's a price to pay, Nicky.'

'I don't care. I am your servant; I lie at your feet. Always.'

'Oh Nicky, my darling Nicky. I crossed a line with you.'

We shared one last kiss. Tears streamed down my face. I pulled away from her for the last time.

'You have to hurry up. They'll be here soon. Should I close my eyes?'

'Yes, baby, and don't open them, no matter what you feel or hear, okay?'

'Okay.'

I closed my eyes. I heard a deep sizzling sound like stitches being ripped from linen, and the floor started to vibrate. I nearly lost my footing but then I felt a tentacle wrap itself around my head, then another tentacle wrapped itself around my waist, and then another one wrapped around my legs. There were more tentacles and they all wrapped themselves tightly around my body. I was struggling to breathe as I was lifted from the ground just as I heard the door crash to the floor. I was lifted horizontally and as I was brought down headfirst, I managed to open one of my eyes between the tentacles that held me in place. I saw rows of salivating teeth, sharp and glistening, with a huge mouth and throat coming towards me. I heard the footsteps of the agents run from the door just as the tentacles guided me past the rows of teeth, to the darkness beyond.

***

'He's waking up, brothers, he's waking up. Give him some space, everyone. Here he comes. Here he comes.'

The voice, deep and authoritative, sounded close but I saw nothing but darkness. It was like I was buried alive. What had happened? I was panicking and my breathing was quick and rushed like I'd just woken from a coma. I reached out in the darkness but felt nothing.

'Take it easy, brother Nicky,' the same voice tried to calm me down.

'Where am I?' I asked. 'And who are you?'

'Who am I? I'm her previous beloved, I guess. We all are. And I think you know where you are.'

'We're inside Princess K?'

'Got it in one, brother. Well done. Where are my manners,' the deep voice said. 'I'm Cyrus. Pleased to meet you.'

'Hi there. I feel there are others around. I can't see them, but I can feel them. You and I aren't the only ones here, are we?'

'Not by a long shot, brother Nicky. There's quite a few in here. Fellas, say hello to our new arrival.'

I heard many voices from all around in the darkness greet me.

'Hi Nicky.'

'Howdy.'

'How you doing, buddy?'

'I should be dead, Cyrus. She was eating me. But I'm not, am I?'

'The version of you that used to exist, doesn't anymore. Our bodies are gone, but it's like our spirit, our essence, our intelligence and our soul remain.'

'So when I thought I was opening my eyes when I woke up …'

'You weren't opening your eyes. You have no eyes. It was your consciousness wakening. We can still see, hear, and we can still talk. We just have no eyes, ears or throat. It's just different. That's the best I can describe it. You live, like we all do, inside the body of Princess K.'

I went to reach down for my Dick Tracy watch. It was gone. There was no letter K that she'd carved into my arm. The arm was gone too, along with my legs, feet and torso.

'Those voices I kept hearing when I was with Princess K, they were you guys warning me off.'

'We were yelling at you, trying to warn you to get away.'

'Even if I heard what you were saying I would have probably stayed.'

'I understand. We all understand, don't we, my brothers.'

There was a chorus of understanding replies.

'How long have you been here?'

'Oh a long time,' Cyrus replied. 'An eternity maybe, with more eternities to go.'

'How long have I been here? How long before I woke up?' I asked.

'Just over a year, my friend.'

'Wow. But why do I have to be consumed?'

'She's invisible. An alien that travels Earth in an invisible form. That's all it is. When she's running low on power, she can be seen. She needs food for power, and she ate as much food as she could, but in the end, it wasn't enough, and that's where you came in, brother Nicky, that's where the rest of us came in. She had to widen her appetite to survive. She draws more power from consuming us and can control her invisibility better afterwards. We've all travelled the same route to get here. That was the closest the agents have ever got to capturing her. That was close.'

I felt miserable. I fell in love with an alien, and I was only a food source to her. I was condemned to many lifetimes of being inside Princess K.

'Does she even know we exist? That we still live inside her?'

'I don't know, brother. She doesn't hear our yelling or our talking. She's never given any sign that she knows we're inside her, still alive. I have a question to ask you. We all want to know, really. We ask everyone when they arrive. What do you think the letter K means? We've never figured it out. Did she tell you?'

Cyrus and the others had been so enamoured and in love with Princess K, no one had worried over trivial details as to what the K stood for. I'd felt the same. But I knew.

'She didn't have to tell me. I thought it was obvious. The K stands for Kindred.'

I heard a thousand audible sighs of realisation from the others. Then Cyrus said, 'The brothers above us are telling me something. There's something they want you to see.'

I felt movement, like people were moving out of their way to make room for me, and I floated upwards. It became lighter, less dense, less dark. I was moving from the centre of Princess K to another part of her.

'You're right behind her eyes, Nicky.' Cyrus had travelled with me. 'You can see everything from there.'

I saw outside. Princess K was in a supermarket. People were walking around her; some were slyly glancing at her beauty as she walked past them. I saw her golden hair flick to the side as she walked to a noticeboard opposite the service desk. I saw her arms and her hands, the same arms and hands that I used to caress.

'She's not invisible anymore,' Cyrus said. 'Her power's going again. The agents will soon be tracking her down.'

I saw a note she was holding in her hands.

> **Alien life form seeking strong man for protection. Contact Princess K.**

I heard Princess K sob as she tacked the note onto the board.

'Oh, Nicky. I miss you, my darling. Please forgive me, please forgive me, baby,' she whispered.

'Oh man, this is tough,' Cyrus said. 'She really liked you. She's been miserable for ages. We could tell.'

'I love you, Princess K,' I shouted to her. The time I'd spent with her was the best of my life. It was worth spending an eternity inside her. I yelled even louder. 'I'll love you forever.'

Princess K didn't hear me. She moved away from the noticeboard and made her way out of the supermarket.

www.ingramcontent.com/pod-product-compliance
Ingram Content Group UK Ltd.
Pitfield, Milton Keynes, MK11 3LW, UK
UKHW041953190726
13854UKWH00005B/1934